T0006912

Other Books by the Author

Manhattan my ass, you're in Oakland (poems)

Virgin Soul (novel)

De Facto Feminism: Essays Straight Outta Oakland (essays)

Homage to the Black Arts Movement: a handbook

The African-American Experience in Four Genres: a handbook

THE HIGH PRICE OF FREEWAYS

Judy Juanita

Livingston Press
The University of West Alabama

ISBN 13: trade paper 978-1-60489-318-2
ISBN 13: hardcover 978-1-60489-319-9
ISBN 13: e-book 978-1-60489-320-5

Library of Congress Control Number 2022935860
Printed on acid-free paper
Printed in the United States of America by
Publishers Graphics

Hardcover binding by: HF Group
Typesetting and page layout: Joe Taylor
Proofreading: Joe Taylor,
Brooke Barger, Jaden Tuck, Ashanti Robertson,
Alexandria McCae, Jarius Hambright
Cover Design: McKenna Darley

Livingston Press is part of The University of West Alabama,
and thereby has non-profit status.
Donations are tax-deductible.
6 5 4 3 21

THE HIGH PRICE OF FREEWAYS

for my dearly beloved mother
Marguerite Juanita Hart
who taught me about the spirits
when I was a girl

THE HIGH PRICE OF FREEWAYS

Table of Contents

MAKING ROOM

When I walked into my bedroom, I saw a little brown boy — cocoa brown, not much hair, big round baby head — playing in front of my son Khiron's picture. He disappeared as soon as I stepped through the door, like he was playing peek-a-boo.

It startled me. I was afraid of seeing "ghosts" — of the dead, again. I hadn't seen one for a while…pretty much since I saw Dad sitting on the chair in Mom's living room, laughing his head off, his hair black and cut to the curl, like when he was on his way to the racetrack. Of course I don't count seeing Raina's mom, who had died in a hospital in Gainesville on Thursday. That Friday I was skimming the freeway to be Raina's friend in her time of need, and a lady in a rickety station wagon, with doors a different color than the car, was in front of me. She looked like she'd stepped out of the kitchen in her slippers to get some milk. As she got off at my exit, she turned her head ever so slightly, and I recognized her as Raina's mom. She drove off and vanished over the crest of the hill —into San Francisco Bay for all I know.

Of course I didn't mention it to Raina. You can't do that. Talk to the relative about seeing the person who just died. They'll think you're off in the head and even be insulted. Anyway, there was the time I told Raina about going out-of-body. About it being a sweltering day and lying on my bed, one minute chilling, the next, a foot above my bed, suspended, begging the spirits to let me down. Which they did after a long while, though the clock had marked only a few minutes.

Raina said that according to what she'd read, out-of-body stuff only happened at death. People don't like to think about the dead or spirits hanging around, even though they say *Jesus Christ* fifty times a day. I stub my toe. *Jesus Christ!* Uncle Sam wants another $400 from me. *Jesus fucking Christ.* Can't you see the no left turn sign, *Jeez-us!* But I'm people too. Seeing the dead can be trying. Life is very comfortable — at least during the day–without consciously making room for the dead. I'm kind of trying not to get back to the little brown boy because he has a history, a life of his own if you will. I will get to him because he has to be heard. The dead are persistent.

My mother taught me about the spirits when I was a girl. She said I was the only one who listened to her stories. My dad called her a Gracie Allen. Gracie was George Burns' wife and straight man. But my mother never meant to be funny. She got very hurt when people laughed at her, and she'd clam up. Whenever she was braiding or pressing my hair, though, she told the stories. Stories about growing up in Oklahoma. About Washington, D.C. where she went after her graduation from college and saw FDR in a parade. About first coming to California and catching the streetcars, and about being the dispatcher in Dad's cab company in Berkeley and the cabbies falling in love with her voice and wanting to take her out until they found out whose wife she was.

She told me about her Papa dying when she was the same age I was then — nine. Papa had caught tuberculosis from walking eight miles in the freezing snow to his laundry job in downtown Muskogee. The family set up his sickbed in the living room so people who had heard he was dying could pay their respects. His last night Grandmother made her go to her room. But my mom told me that in the middle of the night she woke straight up. She saw these little people, the size of children, rotund and nimble and kind of glowing, walk past her bedstead and down the hall to Papa. When they marched back through, Papa was with them. And they were walking but not on the floor — a bit above it.

Of course she doesn't tell this to every Tom, Dick and Harry. My mom's a fifty-years-and-a-gold-watch kind of person. She was one of the first blacks to integrate the civil service — soon as FDR issued Executive Order 8802. She is Missus Solid. She pays parking tickets as soon as she gets them and never U-turns in the middle of the street.

But she knows about the dead.

She used to get these federal credit union loans for when Dad had gambled the money into the Bay, and somehow, the way she told it, it was always a struggle. Would it be approved? Would they give her enough? Would she get to the union office before it closed? I suppose Mom was hurrying in that gray Ford with as much an eye for the loans as Dad had for his horses — Misty Light, Pretty Patty or Rump the Roast — rounding that last lap at Golden Gate Fields. Dad kidded before he died that the only reason their marriage lasted was because they always had two cars.

On one of her trips to the credit union, she encountered someone walking down the stairs as she was going up, Mom with her worried head down, suppliant, thinking I'm sure of our five open mouths, parted like a nest of baby wrens. She said the person bumped into her, causing her to look up for a minute and see that the person was smiling. But Mom was concentrating on the loan. As soon as they passed one another, Mom realized it was a woman with "great big huge upside-down teeth." She looked back. But the woman was gone.

Of course she got the money, cashed the check, fed us, comforted us to sleep, locked my Dad out of the house for the night and thanked the good Lord for the angel on the stairs that had been there to tell her it was all going to work out.

I still look at people's teeth like I'm going to spot divinity there. *Jesus Christ.* Like divinity is a guessing game. I hope it's not. But you do have to be on your toes to keep up with the dead. The ones I've seen move quickly. And, for some reason, I'm usually tired or stressed when they whiz by. I saw Dad streak by in a car down 69th one day, looking like Joe Louis in his prime. It reminded me of how he and Mom argued over money (do married people argue about anything else?) and he backed out of the driveway at 30 mph. Thank goodness no car was coming. When I dream of Dad, he looks like the Brown Bomber. He and Joe favored, even in old age.

Before I tell about the little brown boy, I have to tell my dad's favorite Joe Louis story.

Dad was a Tuskegee Airman, 337th, W.W.II, serving in Italy; Joe Louis back in the states was at his peak as The Brown Bomber. Dad's CO came up with a brilliant idea: get the real Joe and the look-alike Joe in an exhibition bout. Dad went along for a minute. Then, being a bright guy and knowing the real Joe wasn't famous for his smarts, my dad said to himself, what if the real Joe forgets it's a fake fight? Dad bowed out.

The little brown boy playing with Khiron's picture — that's what got me. I keep that picture — one of those 8 ½ by 11 school photos — next to my bedside. Khiron hates it because it's pre-braces. But I love his all-over-the-place smile; I loved that age, nine or ten, before he stopped asking, "right, Mommy?" like I knew everything,

The year before Khiron was born, I was, as we say, "out there" and had an abortion. Legal and all. But I had a hard time deciding to do it, getting a doctor, the whole bit. It was a second trimester. I guess not quite a partial-birth one. But I had to go in the hospital and, in a way, deliver it. They flooded my uterus and basically drowned it, I guess. I remember asking the nurse if it was a boy or girl, and she said in a kindly tone that I didn't need to know. What can I say? I had tried to abort it myself by taking a hundred Carter's little liver pills, contemplated going to Sweden or Mexico (yeah…and my rent was $87 a month), and finally saw a shrink in Berkeley twice who then okayed the procedure. I did it, mourned it, then fell madly in love, married and had Khiron as fast as I could. I picked the name because Chiron is the god of healing. I fell in love with my baby. Adored him. Isn't that what a mother does?

"Welcome to the exquisite pain of parenting an adult," Raina tells me when I complain about Khiron — the loss of contact, the unreturned phone calls, the advice not solicited.

Exquisite pain. Yet here is the little brown boy. Ever since I moved here, I've been buying yin-yang for kids — friends' kids, anybody's kids. I have a yellow rubber ducky on the bathtub, a teddy bear and a wicker chair the height of a ruler next to the window. But my friends bring wine or cheesecake and juicy gossip. I have this picture of brown boys on the wall, playing stickball, going fishing. I cook spaghetti and bean soup – like I used to for Khiron — and throw it away, hoping rats somewhere taste my cooking and rave over it. *Jesus*, I chase enough spiders out of this place. I provide them a home — why not the little brown boy? There's even a little ceramic house on top of the bookcase for him to go in at night and rest his bones. I think the little brown boy is begging me to think of him, too. Somebody said cats spend three-quarters of their time being cats. That's why they don't pay us much mind. Maybe the dead are like that. High maintenance in their own convoluted way…*little brown boy, I'm sorry you didn't get to be loved and live a life like Khiron*…I mean, who else knows that he was playing with Khiron in the picture? Who else remembers? Who else cares?

CABBIE

March 21, 2009. The last day in the life of Lovelle Mixon turned out to be a big holiday in Oakland — the Day of Reparations. Too bad no one knew. Everyone could have prepared, the way they do for Columbus Day or Halloween. Macy's could have sent circulars with 50% off. Even the coolie-hatted immigrants dredging the recycle bins for bottles recognize holidays as an inappropriate time. Too much clamor for the homeowners in the hills (not so deferential to us in the flatlands). Weekdays they make noise, Sundays they let people sleep. Mystically, they know which holidays to trample on. I call it the commotion-sensibility-quotient. For instance, Thanksgiving — they know everyone's too tooted up to be bothered by container-hustlers.

Some newspaper called Mixon a cowboy. He wasn't. Drug cowboys run weed from Arizona and New Mexico up through California. Lovelle Mixon was a gun runner. A dope dealer is an occupation. A gun runner is an occupation. But he didn't make it as a dope dealer. Went to UC, the University of Crime, and found there were several levels open at various levels of criminality. He came out of jail with the ability to make new connections who told him, why you wasting time dealing weed and coke instead of products that move faster and are more profitable. Like guns, illegal weapons, flesh. The new criminal doesn't have to deal dope. Not going to get into gambling, fraud or cyber theft because he's not trained to do that. I intend to put Lovelle Mixon in my book, the before-and-after-I-started-cabbing book. Of course it doesn't exist outside of the parameters of my thick skull. But what a spot it holds there.

New Year's Eve, 2008, my baby brother Terence was broadsided by a hit-and-run as he rounded 66th Ave and Foothill. Crazy fool didn't even stop. Just clipped his Toyota and kept going. Terence's son, my nephew, barely two, was sitting in the back seat, strapped in his car seat. Terence said, "I wouldn't give a damn except that drunk m-f in his Humpty Dumpty-looking Benz coulda killed my kid." When State Farm said they wouldn't pay a dime without him identifying the driver, Terence was so pissed he started a block by block search on his off days. Everyone else carrying on over Oscar Grant getting shot by the BART cop on New Year's Day, except Terence, who was fuming over his car.

It took a few weeks; right after a Martin Luther King Day celebration he spotted it on 74th Ave. Terence said he sat there, angrier by the minute, waiting for the driver to come out. The car, a green Mercedes Benz G55 AMG, was dented on the right passenger side. Some of the maroon paint from the Toyota was on the dent. Like blush on a woman's cheek. Twenty minutes go by. He had to get to work at Kaiser. Nobody came out. Terence said he took down the license plate number. When he reached the corner, he saw through the rear view a burly man come out, walk toward the car and pull off. It was the hit-and-run driver. He wanted to confront him, but he had the license number. He drove back and got the house number, too. I know that house, a notorious drug den. I've picked up fares there. No bueno. Bad actors in and out of that place. I told him, "Don't give your info to the insurance people." But Terence is hard-headed.

He yelled at me, "Man, I'm not paying for what some hopped-up junkie did to my car."

"Listen, lil bro, you mad, you sad, you all that. But if the police or insurance give him your particulars, his crew come by your house, do a drive-by. And they ain't gon be mad or sad, just taking care of biz. No emotion. Just boom, boom, boom, blow you and whoever's in your house away. Forget it. End of discussion."

Bro stewed for two months, like a pressure cooker about to blow if the jiggle top gets popped too soon. He was intent on driving back by the house on 74th Ave. where he saw the Benz. The day he chose to go there was the Day of Reparations.

March 21, 2009. It was after 3 p.m. Terence goes to 74th Ave. and runs into a hundred cops, a crazy scene. He told me there was nothing he could do but stand outside his car and watch. I can't believe he didn't hear about Mixon and the first two cops he shot on the radio. But that's Terence — he goes to work listening to jazz, mows his lawn listening to jazz and watches his kids play, listening to jazz. He's the most predictable guy in Oakland.

By the time Terence got there, the cops were frantic, all over MacArthur Blvd. Terence said it looked like nobody was in charge. The cops started going house to house until they knew Mixon was at 2755-74th Ave. — right in the part of Oakland that is under relentless siege by the po-po. Then they zeroed in, like bees to the queen. That black boy was queen for the day. Otherwise known as a clusterfuck. Terence said it was almost like a party and the people in the streets behind the barricades were talking shit, nearly taking bets on how soon the po-po would go in, like storm troopers. There's no such thing as a standoff in Oakland. We don't have that kind of patience on either side. Either the po-po are gonna let it fly or the target will. This ain't a TV show. *Law and Order*. This is town biz. Terence said the cops were angry and confused and frustrated, all at once, running back and forth. And the street was not even nervous. People were not upset, not hot and bothered.

Terence had been so worked up over his car. But all that dispersed, he said. Right there. Each group of people, police, onlookers — all of East Oakland — turned like a kaleidoscope. He felt like he had taken LSD, and Terence doesn't do drugs, not even Novocaine at the dentist's. But there he was, in the middle of hell with his poker face and, he said, the ghosts of Emmett Till, Nat Turner and Huey Newton looming larger than billboards. He found himself cheering for the brother, for Lovelle

Mixon, for Oaktown, for the convict, for the guy who had murdered a cop, and by the end of the day, would take out four.

March 21, 2009. 1:08 p.m. The first cop that Mixon shot knew him. And knew he was a gun runner. It was a traffic stop by two cops. It's unlikely that they knew his level of desperation. Every cop generally knows on a first name basis the criminals on his beat, and the head criminal knows who's short on the money. All in it together, this one pays this one, that one pays that one. That's why there are so many street deaths in prison. Acts of retribution. I think Mixon was buying time. He wanted to bag up money and weapons. Go to L.A. and disappear. A great many people in the inner cities have no ID, no SSN. They're nonentities. You think you fingerprinted everybody, but you can't fingerprint the entire population. He probably knew that some schemes would lead him back to jail, where he was already a marked man. So that brings up, how did they know precisely where he was and who they had stopped? One of his known refuges was his sister's apt. where the second battle took place.

Incarceration was not the key problem for Mixon. He was attempting to avoid retribution. For an African man from the hood, incarceration is not the worst thing that can happen. Hispanics know it the same way. You find friends, associates, mentors in the prison systems. It's just another neighborhood when you're sent to jail. Leave one hood and go to the next. Three squares and a rack on the inside, three squares on the outside. He didn't kill the first two cops because he was afraid to go to jail. He decided to effect his own retribution. Understanding the end was near, he decided not to depart this world alone. He knew those cops had been sent by his superiors; he was just a pawn in the game now. He was traded off for something else. In dope dealing, how many pimps are killed so that someone can acquire their ho's? In gun running, how many runners are killed so that someone can acquire their product?

In the Warsaw ghetto, how many Jewish husbands were turned in so the snitches could acquire their wives? It's an old story, been going on for hundreds, thousands of years. Squeal on somebody so you can get their land. His death was part of an old script. Not such an individual thing as people thought. The things that didn't add up, though, are who did he know and when did he know them?

March 21, 2009. For people whose Saturday starts at 4 a.m., like mine, that Saturday was a day like any other in Oaktown. Weekend commuters tunneled underneath the stretch of earth called Berkeley-Oakland-Albany-Emeryville-El Cerrito-Richmond-San Leandro-Hayward-Fremont before going into the long submersible BART tunnel in San Francisco Bay. At intervals, the snake pops up and becomes a tour guide through the backside of Oakland and its lower bowel, East Oakland, from which those looking east can glimpse the Mediterranean hillside that runs for eighty miles. Tourists making their way to the airports pass underneath downtown Oakland, speaking in German, French, Japanese, to name a few, about the wine country, the mud baths, the crooked street in San Francisco, navigating its crookedness in rental cars with pedals on the left instead of the right. But they see East Oakland because of Ron Dellums. Or in spite of Ron Dellums. As a young Berkeley city councilman, Dellums argued for putting BART underground so the lovely residents of Berkeley wouldn't have to see the snake crawling through the city. So here's some cabbie wisdom for you: Past, present and future all exist in the same moment. Berkeley got BART underground; every place else aboveground and my man Ron made mayor. Folks like to knock the boss. I don't care white, black, Mexican. Knock, knock, knock. That Dellums, he's sleep at the wheel. Folks, Jerry Brown already sold off downtown Oakland. He said he would get it built up like Rio de Janeiro, tall buildings downtown, flatlands the same. Nothing left for Dellums to do. End of discussion.

People say Lovelle Mixon's going to hell. He killed four people. Hell must be a helluva place. There's death on practically everybody's hands, one way or another. The police chief of Seattle said recently that soldiers follow orders, police officers make decisions, and police officers are not soldiers. Something happened when the police heard the first two cops had been gunned down that Saturday. That's when the clusterfuck started. The Seattle police chief said we're a nation of 300 million guns. When they put on the Kevlar vests, you know the SWAT teams were about to come in the DMZ. The police stopped being police and turned into soldiers. But who was giving them orders?

The po-po, cabbies, neighbors — they all knew 2755-74th Ave. Notorious. Woman found strangled by her own drapery cord. Police know it was her ex, but they classified it as suicide. I never heard of suicide by drapery cord. I rode her around a lot. She could buy out a dollar store with a twenty dollar bill and still have cab fare. She didn't take her own life. Murder, yes. Suicide, no. But the po-po say what's convenient and let the badasses roam wild.

Here's a parable. I call it the Parable of the Two Brothers. Both dead now. Before bro. #2 died, having been drug dealer, user, convict, hustler, parolee, he went around, in his last days, saw his kids, grands, said goodbye. Even went to his social worker, caught up to her on his old stomping grounds, heard her telling a user, "If you can just stop using between tests and not just the day of the tests." Bro. #2 told her, "Scolding won't work. Give him something he can't get out here." She didn't know what that could be. Bro. #2 said, "You can't give money. Drugs. Women. Give him praise. That's what you gave me."

Bro. #1 was dying, same period. Drugs, they shorten your lifespan, don't matter if you're a rock star or a hustler. Bro. #1 hustled me out of $300 twenty years ago. So you could say I'm biased. But in his last days — he had AIDS — he kept traveling to Africa, back and forth, back and forth. Word is he had ladies over there under his ladies' man spell. I didn't buy that. AIDS was so out of control there that he didn't face a stigma.

Bro #1 and bro #2, different paths to the grave, one got more wisdom than the other, but he had done more dirt on the whole. They went to the same six feet under. Which one's going to the crowded place?

March 27, 2009. Here's the definition of awesome. 20,000 police and citizens converging in Oaktown for the funeral of those four dead cops. They came from all over the country.
Even the Royal Canadian Mounted Police. And all 815 OPD attended, according to the SF Chronicle. So who was minding the shop? 15 law-enforcement agencies from Alameda County, CHIPS, and local police departments. Bagpipes, the 21-gun salute from a military cannon, and of course a couple dozen helicopters buzzing overhead, more than the usual four circling the hood. Ah, man, and the OPD told Dellums, shut your black mouth and sit your black ass down. They wouldn't let him speak. If we have to *let* you be here, then be unheard. Word is that the Mayor mispronounced the officers' names at a previous memorial. The PBA didn't want that again.

Yeah, likely story. Remember lynching back in the day? Crackers went for the black middle-class, the shopkeepers, the folks who were coming up in the world. Envy, pure and simple. It's human. But what you do with it is the right or the wrong. One week before 9/11, Colin Powell was at that international conference on racism in South Africa. Said the US wasn't about to apologize for slavery if that apology involved reparations. And the United States delegation got up and walked out, in front of the whole world. What a meathead.

May 5, 2013. I drove a white Lovelle Mixon home one night from the Oakland Arena. Rolling Stones concert. You could hear Mick all the way to the BART station. I went to pick up this white kid, 22 or 23, high as I don't know what. Gets in my cab, and my dispatcher says take him to Sebastopol. Take him where? That's a four hundred dollar ride. His father called in the fare. This kid is high out of his mind, all the way up there. And it's in the middle of nowhere. But we get about a mile from his house. He sobers up enough to give me clear directions. The kid stumbles out. The father pays me double fare, and then pulls out two more hundred dollar bills. And thanks me for my troubles. White, black, same stupid kids, different outcomes.

The guy that's teaching me dispatching says I'll never be unemployed right up to the end of my life because there's always a need for good dispatchers. Back-to-front, dispatchers don't see what cabbies see. Nevertheless, I like security as much as the next guy, and I've seen enough to last.

DRIVING

I'm a bad driver I admit it. My sister came to visit and the first thing she did was she called my mother: "Ziggy still drives crazy AND she's gonna die in a car accident."

That's called sisterly love. At least I never, since I know I talk with my hands, unlike some people, use a cell phone in a car and talk with my hands and call myself driving a car. I'm not that bad a driver. But whenever I'm in a hurry my angels come out to protect me. Whoosh, I'm trying to get somewhere in 5 minutes and it's 10 minutes away. To the rescue Grandma and Grandpa Gefilte Fish magically appear in front of me going 30 mph in a 30 mph zone. How dare they? Aren't you due at the synagogue? Or into my side view mirror come Lin Pao and Miao-Lo. I want to scream. What happened to mah-jongg?

THE BLACK HOUSE

Allwood and I were the only two beings on earth—black guy and black gal in a silver gray beetle crossing the San Francisco-Oakland Bay Bridge—headed for the Black House in the Fillmore in the city rehearsing how to say *hello* and *how are you* in Arabic. We had to be the only two.

"As-salaam-a-laikum," Allwood said, for the umpteenth time, enunciating every syllable.

"Wa-alaikum-as-salaam," I said, trying unsuccessfully to stop myself from saying, "Wall, the lake um's a salami, brother sister baloney, and most high potentate."

Allwood shook his head.

"I'm sorry. I take it back," I said. We entered the city, passing the San Francisco skyline, the offices full of yellow light and reflected dusk. Allwood sighed. The bridge swaying was behind us. We drove to the Fell St. exit and up the hill. We practiced; or I practiced and Allwood corrected me.

When we reached Divisadero St., I broke down. "They won't allow me in if I don't say this exactly right? Who is the boss of Salaam and Sa-laikam, anyway? It sounds like Abbott and Costello meeting up as sheiks on the street."

"Believe it or not," Allwood said, "You're going to like it." We finally parked at Hayes and Broderick. I looked around for a black Victorian.

"I don't see it. I don't see a black house," I said.

"It's not painted black," Allwood said. I came from a big clannish family, had gone to school from elementary through jr. college in Oakland, my solar system. In Oakland, I was at ease. San Francisco was another universe. I waited for Allwood's fingers to direct me. It was a Victorian jammed between two other Victorians. It looked no different from the others except it was a light green between celery and vomit.

"As-salaam-a-laikum," I said to Allwood.

"Wa-alaikum-as-salaam," he said back, ringing the bell.

I was startled. A black man with skin the color of a Hershey and teeth stunningly white stood before us.

Allwood said the Muslim greeting to him.

"Yeah, Brother Allwood," the man said. His voice had a tone that registered so deep it actually rumbled. He took my coat away from me. I wanted to take from him. His tone. His confidence. His beautiful darkness. Something.

"Is this the sister's first time here?" he said to Allwood. I couldn't let him not talk to me.

"As-salaam-a-laikum," I said.

His bushy eyebrows raised.

"I'm Geniece Hightower. I've never been here before."

I extended my hand to him. He looked at it and laughed. More rumbling. Inside me.

"You niggahs from Oakland is quaint," he said. I heard the words "niggers from Oakland" in a way I had never heard anyone say them. Did he sing them? Did his voice go up an octave on "niggahs" and back down on "from Oakland?" His voice, whatever that was coming from his dark neck, was like a boat bobbing on an ocean. I couldn't take my eyes from him.

"This is our fortress against the wolf," he said, leading us up the stairs.

"The wolf?" I felt a quivery knot in the pit of my stomach. Was I afraid or intrigued? He laughed so hard I thought I should stop asking questions. I might hurt something.

"Everybody. The system, the world, the city." he stopped at the top of the stairs and leaned on the railing. "The garbage in the streets, the past, the present, maybe the future."

He raised his coal black eyebrows. "Street niggahs come up with a lot of existential rhetoric too."

"Bibo," Allwood addressed him.

"Your name is Bibo?" I asked. What a crazy sounding name.

"Wanna check my birth certificate?" he said, laughing. When I laughed back, I felt like I was bobbing alongside him.

"Bibo, what time does it start?" Allwood's voice grounded me and jarred me. I had forgotten him.

"The music or the speeches?"

"The speeches."

"Speeches for the good brother Allwood right in there." The brother pointed to a closed door. Allwood squeezed my arm.

I watched, wordless, as Allwood walked in and the door closed behind him. I heard a faint, high-pitched man's voice inside that was overpowered by the smell of this Bibo's body cologne, his personality, by his closeness.

"You belong in here," Bibo said, steering me into a kitchen where a woman was stirring something that smelled like lamb and garlic in a pan. He disappeared down the hall. She was a slight woman, with kumquat-smooth skin, an ankle-length skirt draped on her. Her back formed a graceful arch over the pan, her head wrapped in a purple silk scarf with pencil-thin green stripes. She didn't see me and I didn't want her to turn around and catch me staring at her. The smell of what she was cooking taken together with her appearance was enough. I was hearing the words *Ali Baba and the Forty Thieves* and *as-salaam-alaikum* in a jumble in my head. I felt if I saw her from the front she might spring snakes from the top of her head and twist over and grab me away from myself. No! I wanted to shout out at her. No! You can't have it. I turned and walked down the hall. I wanted to find my friend-boy. Where was Allwood who had gotten me into this? I had to go into one of these rooms. What if, my goodness, I walked in on somebody doing it? All the house parties had a bedroom upstairs where somebody dumb would happen on somebody not so dumb. But this wasn't a house party. This was different. I took a deep breath and opened a door that had a poster of Malcolm X on it. Maybe Allwood would be in here.

"Some people think this is paradise. California: we're free. The South is behind us. Jim Crow is behind us. The ocean is our frontier now. We're a part of the Wild, Wild West ... Don't believe it." The speaker's voice was high-pitched and familiar.

The speaker stood at a podium, two chairs on each side of him. The room had once been a good-sized bedroom but now there were four rows of wooden folding chairs, set up with an aisle about a foot wide. But the room was lopsided because everybody in there was sitting on one side. I wondered whom the other side was reserved for. The men in each chair looked alike, unsmiling with big Afros and creamy brown skin. Did all of these people have clear complexions? Then I realized, as I was escorted with a very gentle but firm hand to the empty side, that the room was full of men. My heart picked up a beat and I became aware of my body, my legs, my jeans that were tight and worn through, showing the inside of my thigh.

"You're not a part of paradise. For you —" the speaker said. Seated where I belonged, on the other side, all by myself, I recognized him from the black radicals outside of City College. "For you," he repeated, with the same rhetorical flourish he used on Grove Street in the middle of the afternoon. "California is paradise with rules, a paradise for fools. And the main rule for niggers, that is, the unschooled fools who still call themselves Negroes, the main rule is —"

He broke off and started laughing. He was tall, gangly, light-complexioned, in fact, pale, like the faded yellow of a man's shirt. In all those lunchtimes I had watched him with the Grove St. orators and taken leaflets for *Fair Play for Cuba* from him, I had never seen him look jive or relaxed. I thought that guys like him had taken a vow to be serious for all the coloreds who had gone before us and been made into hyenas by mean white people. But he was laughing a deep, hearty laugh. I could tell by his entire face and torso shaking that he was really laughing. How could he shake and bellow like that here in this foggy black heart of San Francisco and never have seemed at ease even once in the sunshine and touch-me-I'm-blue skies of Oakland?

"Wait!" The word hit the room like a thunderclap. I started in my seat. I needed to go to the bathroom but even more urgently I needed to get his point. I was following him just like I'd followed the preacher's sermons on those interminable Sunday afternoons. Only then I would wait for the preacher who Uncle Boy-Boy dismissed as ignorant to say something ungrammatical or simple and I'd dismiss the whole sermon. But the Grove St. orators were different. They were book smart.

"That's what the man insists that you do. Wait for justice. Wait for equality. Wait until he gets ready to give you freedom. To give you justice. To hand out equality on a silver platter." The men started clapping. I clapped along with them. They stopped. I put my hands back on my lap.

He cleared his throat like a reverend and went on. I wondered if God awakened him in the middle of the night telling him what the next day's sermon should be. Only his God would be Malcolm X or Marcus Garvey. His God was definitely a black man who wore owly glasses and Big Ben Davis coveralls and carried a briefcase, like he did. And his God then probably was light skinned. All the guys sitting in this room were shades between sand and the shore. Maybe dark me was in the wrong room or maybe that was why I had to sit over here.

" —and then he concocts a rationale for why you have to wait. Not why you should wait, why you gonna wait. Dig it. He gets some Irish cracker — who's probably been to Harlem twice in his whole life — to put together a report and put his name on it.

Yeah, the Moynihan Report —"

This sounded like Allwood's turf.

"Yeah, the Moynihan Report which just means some potato farmer's great grandson is getting over on you, making his name, his rep, paying for his wife to hire your mama to make her dinner and wash her underwear out by hand — yeah, your mother, we know why sistahs' hands be so rough — and sending his kids to a college you couldn't get in if you had straight A's and perfect SATs. I know because I was one of the first Negroes at Harvard. Went in a Negro, invisible and all that shit, came out a black man. Had to. It was either break through to my blackness or die. And you see me standing here."

The men clapped in unison. When I clapped, I broke the oneness.

"Yeah. Moynihan...the very name makes me want to take somebody out. Moynihan says 'the Negro Community' has been forced into a matriarchal structure which, because it's so out of line with the rest of American society — Dig that, you outta-line Negroes, get back in line — he says we 'seriously retard the progress of the group as a whole.'"

I still needed to pee. The walls were lettuce green semi-gloss; somebody had done a nice job on the trim and the windowsills...almost-alabaster. Nice. And I still wanted to find Allwood. But the speaker was up to the clincher here in this bedroom auditorium.

"I don't know bout you but I got a daddy. Fo your ass," he said. "This lame ass white man is your Uncle Sam. And the same mothers and fathers he's disparaging — which is a fancy, white man's way of saying 'putting your ass down,' yeah — those same black people are paying his salary, slaving, paying taxes so the man can write this bullshit, get a Ph.D. off it, and keep you down where you can't even get up and fight cuz you busy trying to prove to him that what he's saying ain't so which he knows already and that's why he puts it out there. So you'll spend the next twenty -five years trying so hard to disprove a lie that it begins to sound like the truth and Moynihan, some potato farmer's great grandson, begins to sound like a prophet."

He was through. I had attended enough church to know that. The men began clapping.

"We don't need no handclapping."

They stopped. "And we don't need no more Jesuses. One was enough to keep us under the yoke for 400 years." Well, I didn't see a collection plate so I got up and slithered out so I wouldn't have to shake hands with the right reverend. But he caught up with me at the door.

"Sistuh," he said. Why did I nod?

"Is this your first time at the Black House?" Could he tell? Wasn't my complexion as clear as everyone else's?

"Don't be embarrassed," he said. Oh, shit, he could read my mind too.

"You're not dressed the way the sisters dress here." He pointed me with his hand on my elbow back to the kitchen. "Fatimah will give you the word. She's a Nubian sister. Queens speak a language only other queens can understand. Dig?"

"Nubian?" I asked.

"Yeah. New Being. Nu-bi-an. That's the word here."

He meant to direct me to the kitchen and I do know about manners but the other side of the house called to me. I heard drums, vibrations, thumping, somebody blowing poetry like a saxophonist was inside his throat. I followed the sounds to a second part of the Black House, another house connected by a passageway. I bobbed along, dealing with a ferocious conga beat. That was when I saw dancers. The first thing I noticed was dark, dark sisters, their hair trimmed and moving with their bodies like fitted caps. It was a dark world and I fit, or so I thought until I looked in the mirror where I saw rolling, twisting torsos around me like serpents. I looked like a Tarzan native on a Hollywood movie set. I looked wild and untamed, countrified. The dancers had sculptured Afros; I had hair all over the place. The dancers had African print draped around them; I had on jeans. It made me think of my family, the side where light people, the high-yellow side, just had to be light. That's all, be light and that's all. The women who were light didn't even have to know how to dance, just be light, which made them pretty. I knew the browner people in the family could be smart as hell, it was never enough. If you were brown, you better know how to do something and do it well. Even then, you didn't get slack. My cousin Clovese had her picture in her paper at work. I could tell she was real proud of it because she showed it around. But I heard my aunt say, "So dark you can hardly see her."

Fatimah stood in the kitchen as if she had been waiting for me all night. I touched my hair instinctively. In front of her, it felt wiry and woolly. She smiled, her face relaxing as if a sentinel had left.

"You are a queen. Beautiful," she said. I didn't know what to say. I had been called cute but dark, sexy but dark, even fine and dark. Not beautiful.

"You've never been called that, have you? A queen?" she asked, her voice soft and rich.

"Never," I said. *Napoleon nose* had been one of my nicknames from the cousins. I knew I had a small waist and pretty feet, my one physically perfect part stuck at the end of my scarred legs. Men had singled out parts, as if the whole me was worth very little but the parts, singly and in pairs, could be worth something at auction. I never believed men who said I was fine because I thought they used the word interchangeably with the thought of wanting to fuck me. The brother who had called her a Nubian woman came to the doorway of the kitchen.

"Tightening her up, huh?" he said.

"Harris," Fatimah's large brown eyes seemed to pour the word out to him. There was something soft and gentle in her tone, the way she said his name. I wondered if she had been cooking for him.

He turned and began talking to someone down the hall. "Let the white kids lead a palace revolt. Let the white man be divided. Divided he falls, united we stand. When the man closes ranks is when we should be alarmed. That's when he's at his deadliest."

He turned back to me and said to Fatimah, "Lumumba, Patrice Lumumba. She's got that same steady look in her eyes. She's got a chilling thing going down in her eyes. Yeah."

My only frame of reference for the word Lumumba was a very dark, dark-as-night boy in high school, with very African features. He was from the South. He wore Big Ben overalls and clunky workingman's shoes and the other kids called him Lumumba. He had a crush on me and my friends had made fun of me because of the way he followed me around. They had called me

Lumumba's wife, which I had hated.

When Harris walked away, I felt free to ask Fatimah. "Am I seeing things wrong here or do I just happen to see mostly light -skinned brothers here with darker-skinned sisters?"

She laughed a tinkly crystal laugh. She was so feminine. I wondered what her hair was like under her scarf.

"You picked up on that, huh? These brothers have an elevated consciousness and, yes, they're trying to prove something. Allwood is your man, right?"

"He's my friend."

Her long, tapered fingers waved like wands at my words.

"Harris, Allwood, our men, our light-skinned men in the movement, they feel deeply about us as sisters, as beautiful black women."

"Isn't that overcompensation?" I asked.

"Maybe you could see it as overcompensation. They want, most people want a mirror. When you look outwardly, unless you look in a mirror, you can't see yourself. You can't see if you're skinny or fat or white or black. You see the people around you. Whatever they are, that's what you feel you are. When you wake in the morning, you wake up human, no age, no color, and no sex until your eye hits either a mirror or another person. Then it's instant. That's who you are — who you sleep with, who you eat with. So I think these brothers have grown to resent being categorized, put down because of their light skin. They're trying to prove who they are inside so they won't be judged by the outside."

I felt a sense of alarm. "Then will they dump the dark -skinned sister once they've made their point?"

She laughed again. "Did Malcolm leave Betty?"

"Malcolm X's wife was dark-skinned?" I asked.

She got a book from a stack on the table and showed me their picture. "Brother Malcolm's overcompensation benefited us all. He became as powerful as we are. He exposed us to our power and that was his power. That's why they had to kill him."

She put the book back and walked behind me. "Let me show you something." With one deft movement of her hands, she twisted my hair, tighter than I had ever twisted it, into a ponytail. She pulled me up and we went to the mirror in the hall. I looked at her hands, at her long smooth fingers, with their white half-moons. They told me my mother had strong fingers with beautiful half-moons.

"Do you see how different you look with your hair off your face?" she asked me.

For so long, I had used my hair as my shield. To see myself in front of her as I saw myself in the morning was a shock.

"You are a beautiful woman," she said, turning my chin from side to side. "Look at your face, your jaw, those beautiful planes of Africanness. Look at the light picking them out. You're a thousand years old. They couldn't beat the African out of you. They couldn't fuck it out."

She wouldn't let go of my head. One hand held my hair tight from my scalp, and her other hand, satin cool, cupped around my chin. "You have to say it," she said.

"Say what?"

"I am such a beautiful woman."

I said it.

"No. Looking at yourself, not me," she said. I said it again slowly, but it was hard not to look at her. She was beautiful.

"You are the one that no one can make unbeautiful. Say it as if it meant all the gold in creation was inside your beauty. Inside you."

I looked at myself in that mirror with her behind me and I saw what she saw. I wasn't only parts put together. I was a whole. She let go of my hair and it went back all over the place. It didn't matter though. I was not just my hair, or my pretty feet that no one ever saw first, or any other part of my body, not even my mind. I was whole and new and she had showed me how to see that.

Bibo came sauntering down the hall. Fatimah watched me as we walked away. He wasn't so overpowering now. We went to another part of the house but he kept talking, pouring poetic shit in my ear.

"Elvis ripped off Big Momma Thornton...The hound dog...Jughead was an agent provocateur for the FBI...Millie the model had silicone implants but we didn't want to hear it...Yeah... *True Romance* tears stop where the real ones start...Ike was a colored man...Dinah Shore's a fugitive from the Negro race...Sammy Davis, Jr. got that empty eye socket from the mob...Little Lotta's fat comes from the diethylstilbestrol in all those hamburgers she stuffs down her fat white gut...Even if we heard it, it would have gone in one ear and out the other...Archie and Veronica freaked on her daddy's bed...You gotta use your imagination, otherwise you'll just be thinking some guy is peeing inside you...Richie Rich made his money from black sugar workers in rural Cuba...Louie Louie was a flasher...Nkrumah has led Ghana into the future fabulous." He walked toward Allwood, who was waiting with his coat on. Allwood looked strange and new too.

"Are you ready?" he asked, one hand on the door.

When we got outside, the cold night air hit my face, right on the spots where Fatimah had held my chin. Allwood was looking down the street at the VW like it was too far. He tucked his chin into his chest. I looked back at the Black House.

"Yeah, I'm finally ready," I said. "Baby, let's go."

The next day, I went to the barbershop and had all my hair cut into a natural.

Sleek, short, very African.

NOT A THROUGH STREET

Week 1

I need help. I can't write down my jokes and routines with all this pain in my arm. The doctor diagnosed a torn rotator cuff, but until I get an MRI, I get no relief — just pain pills, which I detest. But it hurts like hell, especially at night, until my doctor refers me to an Owen Schreib, RPT. Registered physical therapist. An herbalist, acupuncturist, and physiotherapist. When I call Owen Schreib I'm taken aback by an accent I can't place but make an appointment. His brochure says physiotherapy is a professional, highly credible and natural medical treatment option offered to all Canadians to improve quality of life, and its primary focus is the restoration of function. So he's from Canada practicing in California.

I drive up to a ranch house on a quiet cul-de-sac in Kensington, a block from the Berkeley border. When he opens the door, I stumble. He's young and handsome, incredibly handsome. Why didn't he mention this over the phone? That would have been helpful. We sit down and I fill out the history. I'm not embarrassed about age because I look younger. Then he tells me his age. Rapid calculating means I began drinking legally about when he exited the womb. When he asks my occupation, I stumble again. If I say stand-up, I have to explain comedy clubs in San Francisco. He has killer eyes, gray and piercing, that demand an explanation.

"The underground comedy clubs in the city are so far underground they trigger plutonium." He laughs and then says what everyone says. "I got a friend who does that."

Physiotherapy, he explains, is more common outside the States, but he has additional training in acupuncture and as an RPT.

"You checked on the sheet that you have an abnormal amount of dreams?"

"Yes, I dream a lot. Dreams are creative."

"Dreams are critically connected to one's chi." It's spelled xi on his wall diagrams. It's a hot day and I've worn a sleeveless tee. He said to eat beforehand and he'd treat me the first time. He shows me that the acupuncture needles are the size of a sliver of hair, and then inserts about a dozen, with studied gentleness. It's not bad at all. I feel a slight prick once. Then he draws the curtains and leaves the room. The curtains remind me of curtains at the video store that mark the porn videos as off -limits to minors.

"Can you keep the curtains open?" So I can get out of here fast if you come at me. A very handsome man about whom I know very little opens his curtains and leaves me in his secluded house on a secluded street with needles stuck in my right arm and leg.

That night I sleep nine hours; this has not occurred in decades. I am blissfully pain free. Even if he's Ted Bundy back from the dead, I write in my journal, it works.

Week 2

I keep sleeping better, 7 -8 hours. We settle into twice a week, become first-name friendly, Owen and Kit, even though it's odd. Why is this a problem? So what if he's blindingly handsome. It's a rainy Friday afternoon when he comes on to me.

"Kit, what're you doing when you leave here?"

"My rainy day pleasure. I'm going to the movie, not just one, three for the price of one." He knows the multiplex where I scam my way into three different showings. He's going to see *In the Cut* with Meg Ryan. He gives me a look that on any other person I would translate as, let's go together. Dude, you're my alternative physician. You're in my journal. And you're a dude.

"I'm going after work," he says.

"I'm going as soon as I leave here. You have to freebie at the matinee when the security is loose." That evening, after one movie, I look for him, but I'm glad he's not next to me during the sex scene. Full frontal male nudity.

On Tuesday, the first thing I get from him, as he's taking my pulse, "I went to the 7:30 *Mystic River*. I looked for you."

He looked for me? "Did you like it?"

He nods. "But I didn't like seeing it alone, sitting next to strangers." His tone is accusatory. What is his problem? If you can't get a date, buddy boy, looking like that, I'm sorry for you.

"Go see *In the Cut*. It's going to video right away." And

by yourself, since I don't see Meg Ryan movies twice. I have such smart silent answers in my notebook.

Week 3

I start telling people about him, that he looks like Clint Eastwood and that the treatment doesn't hurt. It reminds me of my therapist ten years ago, Dr. Gold, and how I started dressing provocatively for his appointments, even knowing he was gay. I know about transference, where you project wishes, fantasies, and fears onto an ambiguous figure. I'm not doing that. I'm getting healed. He's a healer. So he's a looker — he can't help that.

Standing over my supine body, he seems so tall. When I get up he's only an inch or so taller than I am. It's an illusion. I tell him he looks like Clint Eastwood in his spaghetti western days.

"I haven't heard that since I was in school."

He knows he looks like a movie star, and it's not a jokey resemblance. He's not an easy equation. I reread the brochure trying to make sense of what's going on: physiotherapy, the fourth largest healthcare profession in the world, addresses problems with movement, dysfunction, and pain that can arise from musculoskeletal, neurological, respiratory, and chronic disability conditions, or mental illness and intellectual impairment. Am I impaired or just spellbound?

The next time he looks down to take my pulse, I dare to investigate his face: Ivory-soap skin, unlined except for a faint thread creasing his forehead. But when he inspects my tongue, I notice a thin line of dirt in his fingernails. He's an herbalist — does he grow his own? A health professional with dirty nails?

That keeps infatuation in check for a few visits. This cocky young guy with sideburns. Sideburns, goddamit. My friend Irene with rheumatoid arthritis and ghetto Zen says whenever common mortals approach enlightenment, this devilish function called the Devil of the Sixth Heaven enters the bodies of their relatives or friends to obstruct the light. I tell her about Owen.

"When I leave there I feel like I've been to a male strip club, Irene… the way he rubs my arm from my neck to my fingertips … it's an important meridian he's opening there… do you think it's sexual harassment the way he touches me…the way he presses his index and forefingers around the perimeter of my right breast…and the back rubs are to die for…the first time he unhooked my bra, I said, oh no, he's smooth, baby."

"Fuck him already. He's a ho," Irene says.

"There's something so erotic about him. I think he worked his way through acupuncture school stripping."

"And you keep going?"

"This isn't even half of it."

"He's a ho."

"He does the back rub with a sheet so it's not flesh against flesh. That's professional."

Professional or not, when he finishes the first back rub, the room is so charged erotically, I can't look at him. You're just a punch line, I want to shout, so what if you unhooked my white bra. Thank goodness I didn't have on a black one. Then again, Janet Leigh wore a white bra in *Psycho*.

That night as I drift into sleep, a little guy sits on my leg. He's caressing his head and crying out, "somebody stole my brain." No, you're just a character in my dream. The theft occurred two weeks ago. That night, I try in earnest to bring Owen into my sexual fantasy, but Dirty Harry comes in me instead.

Must be the fingernails.

Week 4

Ramon, who books me, says the doctor-routine worked last night. He's a hound — of course, he liked it. But it's progress to be off my sofa babying my arm. I'm back out.

"I'm paying $367 a month for Blue Cross. Talk about getting screwed [they laugh]. *Health care fucks over everybody. I'm using up every ounce of this three hundred bucks. I've been going to doctors up the yin yang. Internist. Podiatrist. Physiotherapist. Pain doctor. Chiropractor. Dentist. And, you know, I can't figure if it's written in my health plan. But they're all young, white, healthy specimens* [they laugh hard; I haven't even said the punch line]. *Well, one Asian. They all look like sperm donors. I'm spending my days with these guys. I don't* have *a guy. I have a medical A-team* [they titter; no laughter]. *Some days one's trimming my toes and rubbing down my feet. So close I can feel his breath on my metatarsal. The next thing I know my gay chiropractor presses his whole body against my torso, body slams me* [they laugh…why? The body slam movement or the mention of gay and chiropractor in same breath?], *and says, breathe in, breathe out. The resident internist at UCSF finishes examining me and says, If you want, I'll do your g.y.n.exam* [they crack up]. *That'll save you a trip. And up he goes, his long bony digits all over, in and around my outstretched pubis. Who says*

I don't have a guy? I'm promiscuous, the kind of girl you can't bring home to mama. The pain doctor tries to get old school with me, sings snatches of the Tempts in a bass voice as he goes all over my aching shoulder. I can't believe it. I'm getting screwed, serenaded, prestidigitated, unhinged — who says I'm not getting fucked?"

Ramon and I haven't talked since I worked Chico State. When the rotator cuff went south, my perpetual motion stopped. The club scene is like Roto-Rooter; the minute you stand still, you go down the drain. When we run out of small talk, Ramon breathes heavily into the receiver. Does he want me to sleep with him too? Is his asthma acting up? Is he reading something on his desk? I start babbling.

"As usual, the black comics were talking about how much pussy they get. And the white guys were talking about how horny they are. Same old same old." Owen's face flashes by. Is he just another horny white guy? Ramon might be a Texas-grown mix of black, Hispanic, and white, but he thinks black, as in hustle-wary. I run it by him.

"What exactly is bothering you about the guy?

"Like the last appointment, he's wearing a gold chain, his shirt unbuttoned halfway down, and I'm thinking, whoa dude, are you Rocky today or what?"

"What makes you think he's dressing for you?"

"Am I being egocentric?"

"Does the dude have chest hair?"

"In abundance, and it looks good."

Ramon comes through the receiver like Niagara Falls.

"Put this Canadian cracker out of your mind. He ain't nothing but a slim shady."

Week 5

I try. I really try. I tear up the brochure with his picture. I go in, and before treatment, I say what I practiced in the car. "Since I'm feeling and sleeping better, and don't want to do this — you know, doctors and treatments for the rest of my life — don't you think this is enough?"

We're face to face, standing up. His eyes flash with anger. Being this close removes the handsome from his face. Instead, his face is animal-like, stripped of softness, even of its whiteness. My threat of leaving is bringing out some weird animal aggression.

"You're not ready." I forgot I used to like only angry men, thinking they were better in bed, with their bang-me-into-the-wall sex.

"It just seems so indulgent." I'm close enough to kiss him goodbye on the mouth. "I feel like it's pretend. I'm hearing myself say: 'On Tuesdays, I do acupuncture; on Thursday, massage therapy.' That's awful. I'm not some upper middle-class pampered wife."

I'm not the dentist's wife. When I cleaned $350,000 condos for a stretch there, the one that irked the most was the orthodontist's. He was never there, and his blond wife, a post-perky Sandy Duncan, was depressed all the time. I wanted to scream life into her.

Why do I feel fear with him? This is utter bullshit, a situational crush tipped on its side. Meanwhile people are getting blown up in thin air in Israel and Palestine, kids making war with machine guns in Liberia, soldiers with crew cuts and dog tags being blown to smithereens all over, with not even enough left to put in pine boxes; and I'm tripping over this.

"It's not a luxury. And what about your weight?" He's testy, not concerned. During the session, after he's placed the needles, he picks at a whisker under my chin. He must think it's a piece of lint. He picks at it, oblivious to me. Hands off my one white whisker, I want to say. I will pluck it, fuck it. But I don't even roll my eyes at him —I have become afraid of him. Compellingly afraid of mighty whitey.

"You need to come regularlarly." He's going on about this, but what I hear is that twice he says "regularlarly." He's flustered. Is this because I'm leaving, or is it the chunk of Blue Cross payments? Or is that the way they say regularly in Canada?

Week 6

My stepbrother Raj calls and complains about his sprained ankle. When he goes on and on, I tell him about Owen. It's a test. Raj is street smart. He can spot a hustle a mile off. If Schreib is inappropriate, Raj won't miss it.

Raj misses his first appointment. Schreib says he came on the wrong day.

"Oh well," Schreib says about the missed appointment. It's the first time he cups me. Cupping is a small glass globe fired up, then pressed against the skin and popped off after a few minutes. It pulls up stagnant blood. It leaves ugly bruises all over my arm, which hurt me all day. It gives me something to fuss about when I go back. He acts like it's no big deal. What is he, an alien or something? It's painful, dude.

I manage to put my foot down. "You can't cup me again," I say. "It leaves bruises." They look like hickeys.

My next appointment, Raj pulls up as I leave. It's his second visit. He sings Schreib's praises. "I'm feeling 60% less pain." Raj is a cabbie, a smart cabbie who works the airline pilots and ship captains. Numbers are his game. "Your boy is a miracle worker."

I start to put a word in my journal to demystify Schreib, to contraindicate what's happening. SHAPESHIFTER. I try to pull away, but the law of gravity works on his behalf.

Week 7

When I come in now, I'm noticing that Schreib speaks to me in command language: "Take off your top…get on your back… turn on your side." Like he's Houdini and I'm the prancing girl. He could be my pimp, for god's sake. Is bodywork the new jack pimping? He hands me a sheet. I don't know exactly what to do with it. I wrap myself in it and lie face down on the table. After a while, I'm shivering. When he comes back, my teeth are chattering.

"I'm freezing."

He laughs and says in a fiendish voice, "It's called cold therapy."

Is he crazy? I roll my eyes at him. He says, "Just kidding." He turns up the space heater. I'm not even passive-aggressive with him. Am I crazy here? That Saturday, Raj calls me at 8 am. He never calls me at that hour.

"I just slept nine hours. That Owen knows his stuff. I haven't slept like that in years. And he has a great bedside manner." Bedside manner? Later in the weekend I talk with Raj's wife, who's amazed. "Raj is pain-free." She, who doubts everyone from God to politicians to the greengrocer, raves.

Jesus, this was a test; now they're Dr. Dre and Eminem.

Week 8

My arm is getting better. My concentration improves. I go online to traffic school for a $384 stop sign ticket (I forgot. Fine tripled. Sue me). Before the treatments, I tried but couldn't sit at the computer for longer than twenty minutes of traffic school. After two months with Schreib, I sit and do the whole test straight through in five hours. I can hardly wait to tell him.

He asks which online traffic school I used and how much I paid. Then he says, "I did it in two hours. What took you so long?"

I'm dumbfounded. He says, "I didn't read each section. I only doubled-back if I failed the quizzes."

"That means you cheated."

He smiles. "That's not cheating. It's taking a shortcut."

"No it's not. You're a cheater." He's taking great pleasure in this. Ah, another word for him. CHEAT.

I'm not a one-liner, but like Scheherazade, flat on my back I'm at his mercy. I tell more jokes. *How hard was it to find Saddam, a full-grown man buried in the desert under a trap door with an exhaust pipe hooked up to a fig tree?* He laughs, thank goodness. *I went to a singles mixer in Berkeley —first off you see a great mix of Birkenstocks*. I try to refrain from sex stuff, but humor is sex for some of us. *Big breasts are problematic*. He has to tug at my bra to rehook it. *At a party once a man said to me, "you have the nicest breasts in here — can I touch them?" Like they were a pair of Siberian huskies.*

Ramon says I should get a persona and repeat it to myself until it's second nature — that's what successful comics do. So I repeat: I'm an innocent in the whorehouse of life.

Week 9

There are spiders, a daddy longlegs, and a fat black one, on the ceiling. Schreib gets a stepstool and catches them in a tissue and releases them outside. I go into my ants-are-like-a-third-world-country routine. *They have their dictators, their generals, and even suicide bombers — the little brown babies they send out for sugar and water.* I stop because he's explaining the black seeds he's taping onto my ears for pain, anxiety, and weight control. Then he starts tripping off my ears. "Your ear opening is unusually large. That signifies a big brain."

Without warning, he speaks very softly, in a sincere tone, right into that outsize opening, "You know, Kit, you're my best client. Always on time. Never miss your appointments. You do everything I tell you to do. So invested in the process of getting well." CRYPTIC. If all that isn't to say I love you, I am a fly on the wall of my own life.

Deep and getting deeper, this treatment. All the people in the world dying meaningful lives while I live this meaningless life with a handsome, pain-inducing Clint Eastwood look-alike who has the feeling capacity of an alien. He's the pebble in my shoe. A moss-agate pebble.

Week 10

I stretch my hands to the heavens and beg for a sign from God. Oh, please. Who is God but an overweight schlub who sleeps all the time and never returns your calls? I need this to stop but can't take my foot off the gas…maybe the Buddhist gods will answer. I drive to the appointment like a medic with a heart attack victim. I turn right one street too soon. Through the houses on the hill above Schreib's, I see the top of his house. I'm looking between treetops so intently I almost run into a street sign. I stop so close I see the raised metal dots on the mustard-yellow triangle that spell out NOT A THROUGH STREET.

When I park, it's the moment again. I never know what to expect when he opens his front door. His moods are like kegs of dynamite, one day smiling like a Roman candle, the next curt, professional, distant. Today he has a beard, new growth.

"You're growing a beard. Interesting." Covering up something? His hair is a dark lustrous chestnut with no shading, like he's dyeing it. But he couldn't have gotten the beard so precise. UNREAL.

I've looked up transference. Yes, he's become my poppa, mighty whitey. Irene says he's fresh karma. "You're making causes to be connected to his shit, not to him." She's so blunt with her ghetto Zen-Aries self. I don't listen to Aries women — they have no room in their eye sockets. They only see what they see. I know. I'm Aries.

Week 12

All the flowers in the garden outside his house have faces. One is a teddy bear. Just before I knock, I see a white gardenia with fuzzy muff-ears for leaves. Intrigue fills the universe between the knock and the opening of the door. What will be there? Welcome…friendliness…irritation…mood indigo? Is he an ordinary guy caught in my web? Have I dragged him into the whorehouse? Maybe this has to do with losing my balance buddy Gina to Hawaii. She was my shock absorber. We e-mail, but nothing takes the place of a close friend who lives close enough for brunch or a movie.

Schreib and I get to chatting about traveling abroad. When I tell him about my trip to France years ago and then to Singapore, he says, "My girlfriend's from Malaysia." It took him three months to tell me he has a lady. Why is this? TRICKY.

We finish and he comes back in the room as I'm putting my shoe on. The cut of my tank top under my unbuttoned jacket means he gets a birds' eye view of my Marilyn Monroes. I'm bent over and can't straighten up for a second to say, "You're supposed to look away, doc." Instead, I have to put the other shoe on. When I straighten up, I notice he's smiling the grin that makes males look reptilian, or as we say, horny. Another word for my journal. LECH.

I put my jacket collar up. He steps over and starts to turn it down. I rear backwards and keep my hand on my collar, "It's lesbian chic. I like it up."

Driving off, I think: that was hormonal. Is he more male than healer? My girlie friend, Marisa, who is white and goes with black and Hispanic guys exclusively, says white guys don't have game. Feels like game to me. What does Marisa know? She grew up in Beverly Hills and has the smallest waist and big healthy, white-girl legs, which the boys at B.H. High suggested she reduce by surgery. Men. Oh, that's a totally unique word for the journal. MALE.

Week 13

This thing can't be an obsession because I'm not that kind of person. I'm the innocent in the whorehouse. But I'm getting to this touchy point where I can no longer discuss it out loud. I can no longer bring myself to share this. I don't want belittlement. I have lost a marble or two. The next time I go I still wear the tank. After treatment, I button my jacket to my chin like a Victorian lady. He changes focus and asks about my shoes as I lace them.

"What are they?'

"Oxfords." Dude! Plain brown oxfords. "Oh, you mean what kind?"

He nods. Does girlfriend give him enough or what?

"Rockports." I muzzle my mouth. *When I tried them on at the Rockport store in downtown San Francisco, I asked the salesman, are these lesbian shoes? He says, what do you mean? I say, what do you mean, 'what do you mean'? This is San Francisco. Are these lesbian shoes?* The last thing I want is to dive into the sexual pool here. Ungraceful. I get out of his place by the skin of my teeth.

I feel like I'm slithering out of a lair. Does this princely toad know that each of my precious routines is an ingot, a little brick of moral gold? Hard to birth. I hope as I drive off the hill that I never see him again, or at least not until he's old and chunky and his lips have lost their fullness.

Week 14

I'm a bunch of scribbled addenda in the margins of my journal where Schreib's become the main attraction.

Week 15

The crime here is fake seduction, and it's all happening inside a journal. I can't blame him for being a distorted mirror inside the whorehouse. I only see clearly when I leave his house and the light of day floods the scene. As self-help, I envision endings to the story:

—sitting in a Chinese restaurant, Little Shin Shin on Piedmont Avenue, with Gina back from Hawaii on a visit. We're eating our usual-honey walnut prawns and asparagus chicken with oyster sauce. He comes in; he approaches with a goofy alien smile and I throw ice water in his face. How Hollywood.

—crying in a courtroom. I send him to prison for life for sexual harassment. As he shuffles away, his ankles already chafing because prison's no place for white men, I realize he's a nice person. I say, Valley-girl style, "Oh my god, I misjudged you."

—twisting backwards at a yoga class. No longer blindingly handsome, he's gotten pudgy, too pale; the sideburns need clipping. After class, he asks, why did you stop coming? I say, too much sexual tension, embarrassing. He smiles because he knows.

—or show-bizzing my close: *I thought I wasn't fucked up enough to be an entertainer (substitute victim). I thought all entertainers (victims) were either lushes or promiscuous. Then I ventured down Life Street, you know that road where the bulls come rushing through. And I found out there are many more ways to be fucked up than drinking or whoring. So here I am, fucked up enough.*

I talk therapists and acupuncture with Gina via e-mail. She says, "I had an out-of-body experience with my acupuncturist, who is a Jewish woman, and somebody else said hers did an exorcism." Have I become the orthodontist's wife without the dr. on my mailbox?

Schreib and I talk about college. He says he majored in philosophy. "In Logic, I had a professor who flunked a whole class. This triggered such a wave of complaints, including mine, that he changed all the grades."

"An F in Logic for a philosophy major?" This hits my funny bone.

"What's so funny about that?" It's not a rhetorical question; he wants to know. For a day or two I see the quizzical look on his face like the little man who sat on my knee and said somebody stole his brain. I e-mail him:

> *Thanks, Schreib. I got 8 and 1/2 hours of sleep last night due to the treatment. I appreciate your help. Very much. I wanted to apologize for laughing inappropriately at your grade. It's nervous laughter. A friend (who has rheumatoid arthritis and related problems) pointed out recently that I make a joke whenever she tells me about her illnesses. I hadn't realized it until she said so.*
>
> *She and I discussed whether this is cruelty on my part, which she had wondered about. Of course I was horrified that she thought I might be a cruel*

person. Instead I actually think it's due to the tension and anxiety in my life right now.

Actually I got a D in philosophy and have always felt that my knowledge of that subject is a big hole in my learning. So I admire anyone who majored in it.

See you next appt., Kit

The next appointment, I walk in and he's smiling, teeth bared like a crocodile's, standing as if his knees are braced for attack. He could be a crocodile. Really.

"I got your e-mail."

"The queen of anxiety on the throne again," I say.

"I didn't take it personally," he says with a magnanimity that says he did. Raj and Schreib have a nice unproblematic relationship. They talk about baseball hats. Raj falls asleep during the treatments. Asleep? Oh no, I might wake up with him on top of me. My workless (sounds like worthless) days are spent in a reverie of books, CDs, doctor visits, movies — and cooking, since eating out is too costly. Evenings, the open mics and showcases where I come alive, are a carny world: would be jokesters, burnt-out jokers coming off the road to work on new stuff, thirty-somethings worried that Robin Williams is going to drop in and steal their joke, or that he won't drop in and won't rip them off. Into this unreal world rides this Schreib thing.

He's real.

I don't do real. I'm comic. I deal with emanations. He's Darwinian. No, he's not. I'm the one trying to evolve…and finding it's a long process.

Week 16

He has on oversize corduroys, beyond baggy, and a J Crew shirt, XL. Was he fat once? I picture him 80 lbs. heavier with chins and handles. When I take off my pullover, my earrings get tangled. He moves to help me. I jerk away.

"I can do it myself."

He smiles. The face. Today it's Pitiful. The Love-Me face. Next week it'll be Brooding. He does Quizzical very well. I've even seen him do Dedicated. With that much range, he should be a film actor, and out-Clint Clint. Why do he and Raj get along so well? Maybe this is why: about ten years ago, Raj came over, beside himself with anger. He had gotten a letter from a woman he knew in Vietnam. She wrote about the child they had. That wasn't the shock. "We all knew what we left behind in Nam." The woman wanted to relocate to Oakland and needed help. Would he send cash and help her, their daughter, and the daughter's baby find a place? "I have no obligation to any of these people. They're from a time capsule. They're not my people. I was in a fucking war. Go to the Red Cross. Go live in London. Go somewhere else. After 25 years? You think soldier boy wants to be a sugar daddy?" He never mentioned it again.

ENIGMATIC.

I get information online about sexual misconduct and acupuncturists. "Because the healing art of acupuncture requires touching, there is a higher risk that patients will perceive what you do as excessively intrusive, overly intimate, or sexual in nature." I feel relief. There are others like me. I disrobe in private — that's not the problem. And he uses appropriate draping. His flirtatious behavior is the sticking point. I go to the California Acupuncture Board site, which lists a range of sexual misconduct, mapped out by the Medical Council of New Zealand. Like that's going to help. I'm black, not aborigine. The part about sexual transgression, though, hits home: "Inappropriate touching of a patient stopping just short of an overt sexual act may occur with unnecessary breast or genital examinations or trigger point therapy near the breasts or genital areas." He's all over my breasts, copping feels left and right — but it's a turn on, I'm ashamed to say.

I determine once again to make a graceful exit. Why is this so important, being graceful? It is my last, absolute last day. I have been consumed with him. He's driven me nuts. He opens the door, clean-shaven, more Clint than ever. I do treatment, giving him a song and dance about getting a gig in Sacramento that will keep me on the road. Without his beard, he looks honest and caring, professional. He looks stricken that I won't be coming back.

"You can always come back for a tune-up," he says.

Week 17

I write him a dear john: I rewrite it. I hesitate. I stamp it. I keep it for two days. When I send it, that's it. I can't see him again. Ever. I am free at last.

> *Schreib, I want to be honest. I really dreaded coming to our appointments. You have the healing touch and your treatments were effective, perhaps too much so. The dread came from the uneasy feelings stirred*

up by all the touching, the erotic nature of our many interchanges — I just couldn't take it ultimately. Sometimes when I left your house in Kensington, I felt like I had been to a strip club. I went online and I understand that the meridian on my right arm stimulates sexuality or is related to it. But again too much! I came for healing, not sexual healing. I also felt very vulnerable and exposed. Maybe it's the home office with nobody around. I will give you a tip. Someone else who feels like I did, even if it's a misperception, might relate this kind of feeling (he touched my breast, he flirted) to a mate. And that mate might not handle it passively. He (or she) may come up to your office and knock your block off. I'm continuing treatment elsewhere. Any problems I had I take as my responsibility.

My best, Kit

This banishes him from the story of my life. I can never think of his porcelain skin or the touch of his fingers on my flesh. I will forget the slightly asthmatic sound of his breathing. I never have to dip into the gray lakes of his eyes and swim back out. It's finished. I mail it on a Tuesday morning. Wednesday night, he e-mails me:

Dear Kit,
I just received what you sent me in the mail. I'm sorry that you felt uncomfortable after some treat-

ments. I would never be unprofessional with anybody, though I realize doing acupuncture can be quite an intimate and invasive treatment. That is its nature, and it stimulates a lot of energies in the person. I appreciate your comments. It would be terrible to lose you as a patient, and I hope you reconsider coming back.

Take care, Owen.

Goodbye, sweet Schreib. It was not meant to be…oh, who's zooming whom? This is a buyers' market. I get a referral and show up at an office in Berkeley. Right away, the acupuncturist looks like Barbara Hershey with the dark eyes. Is she kooky or quirky? I sit down and look at her wall charts and let out a long sigh. I love white people, absolutely love them. They make going to the movies so worthwhile.

Alas, she doesn't take Blue Cross.

Week 20

I get treated now in downtown Oakland's Chinatown with this wizened Chinese woman who must be 75 and counting, barely five feet, teeth as brown as peanuts, who cups me all over my back and buttocks. Nothing erotic. She looks like the stock Asian characters that played alongside Woody Strode in his glory days.

"The day of my MRI arrives. I go into the city, thinking it'll be like on television, a see-through iron lung. Instead it's closed. I feel like I'm being wheeled into a columbarium. And right before I'm pushed in, the technician gives me a clicker. That's odd, I think, until I'm in there like a sausage with six inch-

es of space above me. My god, a sarcophagus. I'm buried alive for 45 minutes. What if there had been an earthquake in San Francisco and there I am buried alive in a huge wired magnet, tall buildings crashing around me? At least I know how it feels to be an extra in a coffin on a Hollywood set..."

And why actors fall for each other on set — because good looks are blinding.

THE ELEPHANTS: AN OPPRESSION STORY

Well into the 2010s, many black people in California cities tired of whites, Asians and various assorted others moving them out of the urban grid and building high-priced, hi-tech residences. In their tiredness, blacks noticed that the invasioneers came with multitudes of dogs. How would one know that? It became a staple of black comedians on television and in local comedy clubs — white people and their dogs, almost a hack routine. In Oakland, the invasioneers walked these dogs — Pugs, Yorkshire Terriers, robust German Spitzes, shaggy sheepdogs, dignified Afghan Hounds — day and night.

This was irritating in one sense because blacks often felt inconsequential enough having to fend off the forces of gentrification. It infuriated others who felt minimized for another reason: these dogs were treated so tenderly. All, of course, kindly were permitted to urinate and expel detritus at will. Their masters allowed them to stop and smell the flowers and nibble dirt. The sight of a spunky Bichon Frise lovingly waited upon as he assimilated expensive doggie treats triggered something elemental, perhaps genetic, a holdover from the whip and lash of slavery encoded in DNA.

The women of one black book group fumed at this (for them) intellectual dilemma. They owned aging homes in the flatlands of East Oakland and South Berkeley. Their primary financial burdens were poorer relatives who had had to vacate rentals with five-day notices and move far out to towns like Antioch, Stockton and Vallejo. And not the nicer parts of these Joaquin towns. As a nonblack book selection — in an annual nod at diversity — the ladies had read *Guns, Germs and Steel* by Jared Diamond. They found its inevitable link to their own mission when they got to the chapters which theorized why the African continent hadn't prospered in the centuries moving toward the millennium.

It was very simple, though it took hundreds of pages to explicate: the Africans hadn't domesticated lions, tigers, elephants and the like. Unlike the horses, cattle, wolves, sheep on other continents, Diamond argued, the big kills of the savannahs provided food and hide to sustain the hunter/food gatherers for long periods of time.

One woman, incensed at having to drive two hours each way by herself to Manteca for family gatherings, wished the Africans had domesticated the elephant the way dogs had evolved from wolves. Then, she fumed, I could have my baby elephant right here at my feet, no bigger than a Chihuahua. In the spirit of the back-and-forth, one pictured the miniaturized elephant as a service animal. What if Oscar Grant had been accompanied through the Fruitvale BART Station that fateful New Year's Eve by an elephant evolved down to counter oppression? What of an Oakland populated by residents adorned with priceless ivory, a fond memento of a deceased pet? They rhapsodized the fantasy of Oaklanders jogging around its fabulous Lake Merritt with reductive elephants and ivory arm chains instead of imprisoned by slabs of ribs and BBQ sauce and being targeted by irritated whites calling the police on them.

The pragmatic scheduler of the club, whose Oakland hills 3bd/2.5ba was a lucrative Airbnb, had a 90-minute drive to Tracy where she stayed at her daughter's. She quickly put the kibosh on the fulminating by announcing the next month's selection.

But the naysayer/naturalist in the group offered a parting thought: Diamond presents his theory as objective fact; I say predators indulgently turned gifts from nature into beasts of burden while others hunted only out of necessity. We would become the captors and minimizers of one of the world's most incredible natural wonders, the elephant. I grew up with my dad's rat tail Irish Water Spaniel. A delightful dog. Let elephants be elephants.

HOMETOWN

As always, Granny's face was solemn. I thought it came from answering the phone at the funeral parlor when she was young. A girl of seven or eight looking into the face of death a few hours everyday. I knew someone else my age who was raised at a cemetery; her father was the groundskeeper. Her expression, soft and not quite what you'd call dour, didn't vary either. Both were caused, I figured, by similar environments.

We were sitting in Hometown Buffet in San Lorenzo, the noisiest all-you-can-eat place around. I hate it, but Granny loves the stuffing and soft chicken. And cobbler. The little kids dashing around like cars on a freeway drive me batty, but we go there twice a month. The family calls me Granny's favorite, which she shrugs off. "She's got listening ears," she'll say, mostly when she's about to talk my ear off.

After our first plate, Granny said, "I'm going to tell you something I never have told anyone."

I teased Granny about being a closet drama queen. I had to explain it, but midway through, she said, real loud, "I'm not gay," and started talking about the baby she'd had at 15. I guess I sighed — I knew all about it: the secret, the date rape, that it was a girl, that people in the next town had taken it. I got up and brought back cherry cobbler.

"I didn't tell you this. I never told anybody this." The lenses of her eyeglasses magnified the solemn look.

"Lemuel Jackson. Lem. That was the boy's name. We had met at the dance. He wasn't a Muskogee boy." Granny hadn't migrated to Oakland till the war.

"My friends Tessa and Clydie talked me into using my mother's parlor to play cards." Iona, my great-grandmother, was widowed when Granny was nine. So she raised Granny and Sister by herself. She had been a teacher until the Muskogee schools upgraded. "They knew I liked him. They invited him over. We were playing whist and Lem asked me to show him the bathroom. Instead he shoved me into the bedroom and raped me. Very fast. I never saw him again."

I thought it had happened on a date, in a car. I had always pictured Granny helpless and struggling in a Model T., not at home on a bed. This seemed not as rough a plight, even though rape is rape. I asked Granny what Iona said.

"I didn't tell anyone. I was ashamed of it. I was sleeping in Iona's room and she was on the pullout couch in the front room. I just put the teddy pillow on the spot when I made up the bed.

"When did you know you were pregnant?"

"Right away I knew it. I didn't have morning sickness

either. I was too scared to say something to Iona."

In 1929, Iona's husband died of TB and she had to work as a domestic in a downtown hotel. Granny kept a single picture of Iona on her dresser. She looked so strict; I know she wouldn't have approved of cards, especially for girls. Her hard smile and forbidding look reminded me of Lee Van Cleef in the spaghetti westerns. Killer tough.

"Iona was waiting for me to tell her. She knew already from Sister." Who'd gotten pregnant the year before and Granny'd witnessed the at-home abortion. I knew that story well too: the blood, the secrecy, the screams, the infection, and the doctor at the last.

"Sister came forward early enough with hers. I had seen all that blood and never wanted to go through that."

Granny asked me to get her a coffee. Walking back, I looked at how straight her back was, even with the hump of age. It was after two, and the place had cleared out, leaving mostly other seniors and us. The air conditioning had been turned on. Sister — "the smart one" — had gotten a scholarship to Langston University, the black college north of Oklahoma City. I shivered at the thought of Iona staring Granny down every morning before Granny left for work.

"Clydie guessed, but she didn't say a thing, just looked at it every day at school, watching it grow. Finally I told Iona. She was calm. She put her grip down and said, 'We're going to handle this. Don't say a word to anyone. Do you understand me?' I nodded and Iona went to work, and I sat there and cried my heart out. From then on, whenever anyone wasn't around, I cried."

Granny always bragged on how Iona knew everybody, black and white, in Muskogee, how she was a deaconess, how she had her own proverbs *and* the Bible's.

"Well, Iona wasn't perfect, Granny. Didn't you say she used to have a drink at night?"

Granny looked aghast. "She wasn't an alcoholic. She just kept a bottle in the closet to nip on." Her stash, her stash, I said in my head.

"Muskogee was full of black people, and while we didn't associate with white people, even the poor blacks were snooty. Now go up and get me a heel, Sweets."

I frowned. "The food's all picked over, Granny."

"Oh, don't I know it, but the children throw back the heel. That's why I love it. Nobody wants it but me."

"That's enough to turn my stomach."

"Scoot your up-turned stomach up there. And don't forget the butter."

I placed two ends of white bread and two pats of butter before her.

"Mother took me to the doctor. And after he examined me, he said to Mother, 'What makes you think she was raped?' And Mother said, 'I wasn't there. I didn't see it. But my bed was used for raping my child. How do I know? Because the bed-spread had a blood spot the size of an orange.' "

Granny smiled. "Up until then I thought Mother didn't believe me."

The help, all young and mostly Latino, sat at one end of the room. Granny started nibbling on a heel.

"Mother had a friend in Sand Springs — Miss Jessie —

who'd been in a bad marriage, and when it broke up, Mother let her live with us. So Mother arranged for me to stay with Miss Jessie through the delivery. When time came — seven and a half months — Mother put me on a bus, bright and early in the morn, for Sand Springs."

Granny was getting agitated. "She gave me instructions. '*The bus will go through Tulsa. Stay on it. Don't get off. Get off in Sand Springs. Go straight to Miss Jessie's. She lives a block and a half straight down from the station. Stay inside Miss Jessie's and don't bother nobody. When you have it, you're going to stay for three days. Get on your feet. Miss Jessie will put you back on the bus. Do not bring it back with you. Do you understand me?*' And then she repeated everything."

Granny looked around, as if some thought was coming to her. "Sweets, go get Granny's Jell-O, please."

I went up and put three cubes in a saucer. Granny was standing when I got back.

"Are you ready to go?"

"Stretching, child." She sat down. "You know that ride to Sand Springs took a long while. Muskogee was a city. I was a city girl. We passed those little towns along the Arkansas River. First, Taft, where they had the mental hospital. Then Red Bird. Colored lived there, and Bixby. That long stretch of the Arkansas had me to thinking of Poppa. He'd go fishing there. Drive his four-door Ford in the summer without the windows. He kept the windows put away — all canvas, plastic and snaps. And we'd snap them off. Every piece of window had a snap." She sighed. It was a good memory for Granny. She told me before that Poppa stuck up for her and that he'd been gentle.

"They had high ideals," she said. "Poor folks didn't just sit around and be pitiful in those days. When I got to the town, I went straight to Miss Jessie's. She had a one-bedroom house so she put me up a cot in her room. Mostly though she was up at her white folks working. I had my orders not to go anywhere. She'd cook, put it in the icebox, and I'd eat off it for two or three days. I was there by myself most of the time. I'd been told not to ask any questions and not to tell any of my business.

"Now the ice man came by every day. I'd get 25¢ worth of ice to last two days. Miss Jessie cooked fried chicken, peas, and beans. I made the cornbread."

I felt so bad for Granny – all alone and so naive – and I got mad at Iona.

"There were four women who lived alongside Miss Jessie and they were told to look in on me. The woman two doors down took a real interest in me. Gave me ripe bananas. She wanted a baby real bad. She said to me, 'I like to have your baby. You can just give it to me when you spit it out.' I wanted to spit out the whole story, but I kept it inside.

"When my water broke, I called her and she called Miss Jessie who came right down. She had me to lie on my back and take my panties off. Then she said, 'There's nothing anybody can do right now. You're going to get these pains. Just grunt real hard to bring the baby's head down.' By time the other women came, it was out. They all washed it and by then the doctor from Sand Springs, or Tulsa I guess, got there. He cut the cord, examined it, and complimented the women. I gave him the money Mother had given me — it wasn't but about $20 — and out he went. I named her Cora Lynn. She had a beautiful high brown color and chubby cheeks, like Lem. The woman that gave me the bananas took it. July 13, 1936, I believe."

We both sighed. The room had cleared. The help had finished lunch.

"I knew what I had to do. I was to pack my things and get back to Muskogee as soon as possible. I stayed in bed for three days and then I caught the evening bus out of Sand Springs and I was glad to go. I had to finish school and get into Langston."

We walked out of the all-you-can-eat buffet. I unlocked the car for Granny.

"As slow as the ride there was, that's how fast it was going back. Those towns whizzed by. Pitch black outside. Each time I tried to think of it, I couldn't. It was like the dark covered everything, even inside my head."

Granny and I were on 880 headed back to Oakland, ahead of the commute traffic. "All these lights and neon signs. Drive the Nimitz anytime and it's still all lit up. Iona met me at the bus station. She grilled me. '*Did you do this? Did you do that'* And I nodded where I was to nod and shook my head where to shake. Iona never mentioned it again. Sister never mentioned it at all. And I never saw Miss Jessie again."

I stayed in the slow lane like Granny preferred. I glanced at her to see if telling the story had relieved her. "How are you feeling, Granny?"

"I have a pain in my chest."

"Where in your chest?" I knew Granny was taking lopressor for her arrhythmia.

"In my heart." She touched the center of her chest.

"How long have you been feeling it?" I debated pulling over.

"Since I finished telling you. Feels like a little knife cutting a piece out for somebody to chew on."

We were halfway between Kaiser Hospital in north Oakland and the one in Hayward. "Should we go to Kaiser?"

"No, no, it's going away. I made myself forget it. It's not painful. I was underage. I had to do what I was told. I'll be okay." We passed the Oakland city line. "Hometown's chicken tastes like the chicken up in Reno."

I sped up because I was out of the suburbs. Granny told me to slow down.

"One time in that sixty years I was standing on a street corner in Oakland. A woman who would have been her age and coloring stared at me hard. So hard I thought back to Sand Springs." Granny rocked back in the seat like church, the part where the preacher gives the call. "Iona did the best she could."

When we got to Granny's senior apartment complex, she turned. Very sternly, she said, "Now that I've told you, I don't want to discuss it again."

I nodded. I walked Granny to her elevator. I went to push the button and she put her hand on mine. "I want to eat this before I go up." She pulled a napkin out of her purse and munched on a heel. When she finished, she wiped her mouth with the napkin from the buffet. She balled it up tightly. Then she balled it up again tighter, like it was clay and she was making it perfectly round.

"Since I told you everything, I might as well tell you this too, Sweets. I saw him once again. At Langston. I was with a friend and she asked me why this boy was looking at us so hard. I turned and saw it was him. He was staring at me. I told her, 'He's not going to bother us. Don't worry.' And he turned and went in the other direction and I never saw him again."

We went up and got Granny settled in. When I said goodbye, Granny's expression looked dead on Iona's. Spitting.

Then Granny smiled, and her face went soft and solemn as always.

Miss Bronze California 1966

For years, beer, wine, and liquor sponsors had showcased a colored people's Miss California contest. Its mostly light-skinned beauties decorated alcohol posters at black businesses, bars, dry cleaners and Laundromats. I'd seen my share at on-every-other-corner beauty shops. I had heard that Deidre McDonald — the only daughter of Oakland's most prominent black architect — perpetually celebrated being Miss Bronze California 1963. I hesitated going to her party after the contest. The evening had been a nonstop immersion in sequins, eye shadow, phoniness — phony smiles, model poses with the tangled feet, mimicked answers one after another. One high yellow feast was enough. But covering the pageant included checking out the party.

Entering Deidre McDonald's plushy apartment overlooking Lake Merritt in downtown Oakland, the first thing that caught my eye was the blue vein crossing her cream-colored instep encased in a white pump with a three-inch heel. The womanliness of her white pumps was positioned like a sentinel against the zip and shine of my new boots. The second thing that caught my eye was her Paul Newman wallpaper. Someone had blown up a black-and-white photo of Paul Newman until his head was bigger than a Goodyear tire and plastered the wall with it.

Deidre McDonald had been at the hall emceeing the evening: *We're passing the baton of beauty on to a new generation of young women. Miss Bronze California, the contest that I was so proud to represent, has changed with the times. The community and we have thrown our support behind the new Miss Black California contest...unequivocally.* She had sounded as if she was reading from a prepared text. But nevertheless that was the moment bronze turned to black.

We proudly honor the beautiful young women here as much for their intellectual accomplishments as for their varied beauty...we've heard two fine piano selections, a jazz rendition, three dramatic renditions, and... She paused there and cleared her throat, as if, I'd sensed, she was trying not to say what would have been unthinkable in years past: ... *a wonderful renditions of African dance — that we all know is our heritage as taught by the beautiful Katherine Dunham.*

Every part of her life, every smile she served up, had been based on being light and bright. Now she was being told to move over and make room for her darker sister. But she was going out graciously.

I had a press pass but had given my uncle and aunt a pair of $15 tickets because I thought he would be tickled and my aunt pleased. Early on, my uncle said in a whisper loud enough for everyone around us to hear, "That girl's got an overbite...she doesn't need a new Impala...she needs a referral to an orthodontist."

"They're not giving away an Impala," I whispered. "First prize is a Mustang. What happened to *yay-us*?" *Yay-us* was his favorite saying to cheer on any black person against the odds. He screwed up his face, "Yay-us? This ain't yay-nobody. It's Pete-and-repeat." My aunt shushed us both.

Within the confines of her foyer, my eye pulled away from Deidre McDonald's white plush carpeting and blue-veined foot as she gave me the once over. Her eyes, lovely, bright and cold, passed me over, head to toe. I felt conscious of my skin, as though her eyes had fingertips that skimmed my forehead, arms, legs — all the exposed parts. She finished her assessment and broke a smile. She didn't need false eyelashes.

"I'm from *The Tower* at Oakland City College."

"I hope you got good pictures of the girls. Some of them go to City."

"I'm not the photographer."

"What do you do?" Good question, honey baby. What do I do? *I doodoo*. Her thin nostrils flared as if she heard my thoughts.

"I'm a journalism student."

"Then give us a good write-up...more than a caption, sweetie."

She walked past me to circulate. I felt a strong urge to shout at her, to get her to pay attention to what I had to say, to look into her eyes, to see a small reflection of my face in the corner of her pupil.

Instead I drank two rum and cokes and partied hard. I knew how to do that. I could fake the moves...for a while.

When we started footstomping on Deidre McDonald's fancy Lake Merritt apartment floors, she pulled up the needle and said, "This ain't the funky four corners. I have neighbors, people."

I danced one slow side with a heavy-set guy — one of the Oakland Raiders there — who breathed hard and pushed my pelvis to his. I felt the zipper of his pants against my skirt and him swell against me. On cue, I was supposed to grind back, push my body into the envelope of his arms, and let him lick it shut. Splib alchemy. I disengaged myself as politely, as sweetly as I could. He shrugged his shoulders. I knew he wouldn't follow me.

I went and sat down on the steps leading to the bedroom and watched the party with one eye and the Paul Newman wall with the other. His blown-up eyes got creepier. Glinting and wide, they stared at the party, the room, her back, and me. Inconspicuously, on my behind, I slid upward to the top of the steps crunching a handful of salted mixed nuts. But Paul Newman's eyes could look wherever they wanted, not miss out on anyone. They followed me up the steps. His mouth, with its two thin lips now as wide as manhole covers, wasn't so bothersome. The eyes, they had the power to condemn. They were saying *Why you sitting there? Why you moving farther and farther away from the dancing? Why you here if you're not joining in? Why you slinking up the stairs? Don't you know women slink down stairs not up? You trying to slink on your butt like Eartha Kitt?*

I slunk farther up the stairs until I got to the top and couldn't see the eyes or the party. Munching peanuts, I watched a couple going past me into the bedroom. They put their coats on and went back out, leaving the door ajar. I went in.

Through her bedroom window, I saw Lake Merritt glistening in the dark, the brand new Kaiser Building looking like a cake knife slicing the navy blue night. I saw the Children's Fairyland sign that I had seen often and up close as a child. In an alcove, I also saw my reflection in a window that faced the bed. I walked around the bed, the coats, and the mirrored dresser with Deidre's makeup, powders, perfumes.

I walked into the alcove. It was set up as a study — desk, bookshelves, chair. I looked at the pictures in frames serving as bookends. Photographs of Deidre in a swimsuit, a ballet tutu, prom gown, beach towel, suit, sundress, and Pendleton skirt. And baby photos — one in what looked like her mother's arms, one in nothing, one with a teddy bear. The smile changed from picture to picture but her eyes stayed the same.

I heard the dancing and the music change from slow to fast sides. The party pushed into itself. I looked at her books. Each one I picked up had her name engraved on a slip of flowery-edged paper inside the front cover: *The Red Badge of Courage, By Love Possessed, Of Mice and Men, Look Homeward, Angel: A Story of the Buried Life, The Return of the Native*. I pulled that one out and began to read, skipping from one underlined section to another, sitting on the floor next to the small sofa. When people came to get their coats, I could see them in the window but they couldn't see me. I was fascinated by what she had underlined, by the fact that she'd read it and I hadn't. A couple came into the bedroom; I heard a male voice. The door locked.

"I been watching you all night."

"Oh no you haven't."

"Oh yes I have."

I felt myself shrinking into my body. I looked at the Kaiser building, imagining it piercing the night like a knife. I heard them kissing. A dress unzipping. I was afraid to search for their reflection in the window. I looked down at the book. I didn't want to see what I was hearing. I couldn't turn from pg. 35 for fear they would hear me:

> Persons with any weight of character carry, like planets, their atmospheres along with them in their orbits. And the matron who entered now upon the scene could, and usually did, bring her own tone into a company. Her normal manner among the heathfolk had that reticence which results from the consciousness of superior communicative power. But the effect of coming into society and light after lonely wandering in darkness is a sociability in the comer above its usual pitch, expressed in the features even more than in the words.

I heard them fall onto the bed. I read the passage again.

"My husband's right downstairs."

"You too young to have a husband."

"I know."

I looked at the window to see how old she was. I saw the Children's Fairyland sign. I remembered that Walt Disney visiting it had gotten the idea for Disneyland. I saw coats on the bed moving. They had sunk into the coats. I heard them. I looked down at my book.

"I've never done this before," she said. I looked up. In the mirrored reflection in the window I saw that she had long hair and light skin. She had taken off her bra. He was buried in the coats. She moved up and down, her panties on. I looked down.

"Come on baby. You'll never forget this." Why do they always say that?

"I've never cheated on my husband." As if her voice had a string tied to my neck, I looked up. Her panties were off. I looked back down.

"This ain't cheating."

Close to my ear, bedsprings squeaked. They seemed to be moving in time to the music downstairs. I wanted not to look, but I saw his hands, large, muscular, dark brown, spread around her buttocks. They started to come. She let out a loud sigh. They both started laughing. I looked away. I looked back. She got up. He got up. He pulled his pants back up. She grabbed the side of the bedspread and wiped herself.

"One more for the road," he said.

"You're a bad boy."

"Ain't no boy inside this."

"A very bad boy."

"Pull up your dress."

I couldn't see them. I heard them gasping for breath. I couldn't tell if they were standing up or pressing against the wall. I heard someone knocking on the door.

"Hurry up. Finish," she said. They came again; I heard them start to laugh quickly. I felt like laughing too. Whoever was banging on the door had walked away. The two of them left the room. I imagined their faces. I put Deidre McDonald's book away and walked into the room. The door was ajar. I came out. A girl about 19 gave me a dirty look and pushed past me. I rejoined the party.

I looked for the couple, but it was darker now downstairs. When I left, Deidre McDonald showed me out.

"Thanks for coming to my party. Did you enjoy yourself?"

She seemed as if she wanted me to answer. But then she smiled at someone else and closed the door. I walked the stairs outside the building instead of taking the elevator, letting the darkness touch me a different way as I stepped onto each concrete pad. It wasn't until the night air hit me that I felt it, her shutting the door in my face. That plush white, dark white world in her apartment was the Top of the Mark.

The close-knit orb of my growing up swirled in my head. Sunday school, violin lessons, Girl Scouts, the colored — barely -black world that had taught me its strict sense of place, its strict and absolute relation to the great white world surrounding it. The closest I had come to daring were the Friday afternoons when my cousin, she lugging her viola, and I, carrying my violin, cut class, and rode the bus to the main library across from the Alameda County Courthouse, sneaked in *Laura Scudder's* potato chips and *Mother's* oatmeal cookies and sodas, all to swoon in the utter rapture of Schubert's *Rosamunde*.

My Mary McCloud Bethune speech during Negro History Week — the exact same words year to year if I found nothing new in the library — was as close as I had ever come to formal blackness. The rest had been a womb that had held me in tightly.

I had come from the top of that world — Paul Newman's face and a fancy apartment. The heights. I stood at the bottom, across the street from Lake Merritt in all its dark watery shine. If it swallowed me, my boots would become mermaid scales, and I'd float through San Francisco Bay, past the thumb of the city and out into the Pacific. It wasn't a frightening thought. Looking towards San Francisco I saw a faint glow beyond the Oakland skyline that comforted me. Night's darkness, with its aureoles of imprecise yellow, shimmering gold and flat clay ochre, was my protector. I could turn to it when I had nowhere else to go.

BETWEEN GENERAL MACARTHUR AND ADMIRAL NIMITZ

Stacie Barber Blake married Clifford Gibson in the backyard of her home on Golf Links Road on Memorial Day. Etta James' ballad, "At Last," played as the bride walked down the grass wedding aisle in an off-white pantsuit with a lace bustier. Her split-level house sat on a hill above the juncture of the MacArthur and Warren freeways, and the guests, all twelve of them, intermittently watched the bride and groom get lovey -dovey and the cars buzz by toward downtown Oakland or suburban San Leandro. The preacher left as soon as Stacie's father, a tall, broad-shouldered black man in a crisp linen shirt and slacks, slipped him the envelope.

"How much money did your dad give him?" Don Milton asked Bern Barber.

"Knowing Daddy, a thank you card. Maybe."

"You kidding?"

"He put two 20s in it. I saw him when he put it in, with

his Bible-reading, wannabe-a-preacher self."

Don Milton sat down. "I have to sit, Bern." He adjusted his empty left pant leg. The lightweight wool had been folded and pinned neatly above where the kneecap had been. Bern popped back up and headed for the glass-topped picnic table with the food. She surveyed it boldly and came back. Don Milton grinned at her. He had small white neat teeth and smiled constantly.

"What you trying to prove?"

"I had to see what Stacie tried to set up for food. Tight as Miss Thang is, I wouldn't have put Taco Bell past her."

"Bern, you jealous."

"If I'm jealous, tell God to put your leg back on. Anytime somebody marries four times, I'm sorry. She thinks she's Liz Taylor. Four times, one annulment, and the only one worth something was Phil, and he died. She could have varied that shit, like live with somebody. No, Miss Thang must have a wedding each time."

They could see the San Francisco skyline and the flatlands of the Eastbay from the hilltop backyard. Stacie's longtime realtor had sold her the house at a steal because it was directly over the Fault. Stacie had snatched up the five-bedroom, three-bath house, and filled it with antiques and Aunt Jemima, Uncle Ben, and Little Black Sambo memorabilia.

Bern lived in the San Leandro flatlands and the Barbers lived in East Oakland, a stone's throw from the 880 freeway. Mr. Barber still called the 880, 580 and 13 by their maiden names. Nimitz, for Admiral Chester Nimitz, was the workhorse freeway, replete with groaning, smoking, speeding eighteen-wheelers.

Hillside residents voted to keep the busy MacArthur freeway, named for General Douglas MacArthur, free of heavy trucks and buses. The Warren, often enshrouded in high fog, cut through the city's exclusive skyline homes. In fact, all three households were near the Hayward Fault. When an earthquake occurred, Mr. Barber used a conference call to check on his daughters.

"Every time I drive the Warren, I laugh at how that old coot fooled Ike," he informed Don Milton. "Ike promised Warren the Supreme Court appointment if he would drop his bid to be president. But Warren double-crossed him by upholding Brown versus the Board of Education. He got that ball rolling for integration."

Bern piled two earthenware plates with skewers of yakatori chicken, shrimp, shish kabobs, spinach-stuffed mushrooms and asparagus spears. As she poured two stems of champagne, her father walked over to help her carry it all and whispered to her.

"Betcha — how long?"

"Daddy, you know that's pitiful." Bern looked at Clifford, the groom, and back at her father. "OK, six months. But what's her point? That's what I want to know. Why does she keep doing this?"

Her father had a hearty laugh. "It takes a strong woman to keep on keeping on."

Bern went back and picked the plumpest chocolate-dripped strawberries. "I'm strong too. But I don't believe in marriage. It's a prison that people voluntarily walk into. They commit the crime of lust, and out of Christian guilt, they sentence themselves to marriage. And they have to get a judge to get out? Oh, no."

"Give Don Milton those while I go get my plate," Mr. Barber said, taking the plate of berries.

"Don Milton is case in point."

Don Milton had been her hairdresser before he got sick. Bern had strolled into his little shop near Lake Merritt one day by chance. They became instant friends, her two-hour biweekly appointments a time for history — personal, hurtful — to flow through the medium of his fingers and her hair. His wife, who had been a hair model, had stayed with him through the biopsy and exploratory surgery, but left after the amputation, taking their baby girl.

"Bern says marriage is a prison, Don Milton." Mr. Barber sat down next to him, relishing the chicken, sliding it bite by bite off the long pick, talking and chewing. "Now you know I been married 47 years. Through thick and thin, the rooster and the hen. I wouldn't know the inside of a prison if I saw one."

He gazed with fondness at the bride and groom posing over the cake for the photographer, their hands joined on the knife.

Don Milton was working his way methodically through the chicken, the shrimp and the asparagus on his plate. "Testify, Mr. Barber. You got a honey and you know it."

Mr. Barber got up to take a picture with Stacie and Clifford. Don Milton turned to Bern. "Your mom keeps her nails done, and her hair. I bet she gets pedicures."

"She gets it all. She better. My daddy's eight years younger than she is. Somebody come along and snatch that younger man like she snatched him from his first wife way back in Mississippi."

"Your family's a trip. Thanks for inviting me. I see you the daddygirl and Stacie mommy's baby. She petite, you thick, but both y'all got it going on."

"I'm my father's only child. He might have raised Stacie but I'm his only natural child."

"And that's what makes you special, Bern?"

At the start of the Fourth of July weekend, Stacie stopped by Bern's to go food shopping. Bern lived in a garden apartment complex on Haas off East 14th, near City Hall. It had been exclusively white thirty years ago — like San Leandro. Bern's neighbors now were black, Latino, white. Across the street, a pair of more-or-less discreet drug dealers lived.

"Where's your makeup?" Stacie called foundation and eyeliner face panties. *Gotta put my panties on*, she liked to say. "You only wear no makeup when you ain't got no man," Bern observed.

"Don't worry about it. When did you have a man last? You might have to wear one of those badges the checkers in Safeway wear. *Been here since nineteen whatever sitting on it.*"

They took Bern's Rabbit the four blocks to the Safeway on their way to the upholsterer because the footstools were in the Lexus trunk. They parked in front of Round Table Pizza and walked past a black homeless man who extended a tambourine. Bern kept walking. Stacie dropped in change that clunked against the drumhead. Bern waited until they were out of earshot.

"Don't you think it's insulting to give him your spare change? If you're going to give him money, give him dollars."

Stacie stopped walking. "I don't want to give him anything. I hate to see black people begging, especially in San Leandro. Twenty years ago we couldn't live here. Now we beg here. That's not progress."

They walked down the paper goods aisle together.

"What I'd like to do is drop him in a tub with some baking soda and scrub him down, like Momma used to do us," Bern laughed. "Bathe him, read him a story, and make him recite the Lord 's Prayer. That would cure his homelessness."

"Momma was trying to scrub the black off us, don't you think? She'd scrub so hard my skin would be ringing until I fell asleep. That's pathetic."

"Yeah, but one week and he'd be a whole different shade."

They split up and met back at the register. After the items passed over the barcode reader, they split the twofers – chicken, sliced turkey breast, Tide, napkins, Dove soap, Crest toothpaste, corn flakes, wheat bread, margarine, hominy grits, blackeye peas. As they were bagging, Bern stopped. "Oh, I forgot, I'm going vegetarian. I don't want the meat."

"Vegetarian, Bern? You think you'll last the month?"

Bern sucked her teeth. "Just because you don't have faith in me doesn't mean I don't. Meat is toxic."

Stacie snarled, "First you gave up men. What's next, an electric car?"

"I'm not celibate. I just said no more married men. They're like a drug. And I was addicted."

"If it weren't for married men, sometimes, I would have had no men at all," Stacie said. "Thank God for married men."

"Somebody should give me a Medal of Honor for not creeping. Plus, taking somebody's husband is a bad cause."

"It's combat duty in the battle of the sexes."

"Nigguhs love to do that kind of shit just to pass the time of day," Bern gunned the engine at the stoplight.

"Speaking of passing the time, where is your friend? You two are tight as girlfriends."

"I was going to suggest we go and visit him at Highland Hospital. Want to come with me?" Bern passed Haas and took Estudillo toward the MacArthur freeway.

"Highland. Is he sick? Where are you going? I don't feel like visiting the sick today. That's not what I'm in the mood for." Stacie closed her window and flicked on the air conditioning.

"You're the best advertisement for why black people don't need to get a college education."

"It's too painful to be around somebody like that. How does he stand it anyway?"

They passed several blocks of well-tended homes with precisely guttered lawns, then Walgreen's, and a new coffee-house. A man in shorts and sandals carried a latte container to his car.

"Yuppie!" Stacie squawked. "San Francisco too much for you? You had to come to San Leandro? It's not white any-more. My sister's on unemployment right next door to you."

Oblivious, juggling his latte and keys, he got in his car,.

"Okay, let's go see the brother. John Milton."

"It's *Don* Milton."

"Same difference."

Maurice was the first. Bern had been working at the floral shop in the BART concourse in the city. He caught the same train every morning and flirted with her silently for weeks. He started speaking after the one day transit strike. It touched her, as if he'd missed her. When he asked her out, she didn't want to pretend she wasn't interested. Only after they were intimate did he break the news. The second was Antoine who lived in her old building. She knew from jump his wife was stepping out and a coke fiend. That made it all right, even necessary for a while. Three was the clincher. Arterberry. The dream man. Tall, dark, not quite handsome, suave, into roses by the dozen, Godiva chocolates and candlelight dinners on the waterfront. She had fallen for it all, gulped it down like a baby at the breast, choosing to believe in the pending divorce. He had given her money too, $600 once when she needed it, fifty liberally. Maurice, she gave a few weeks of her life; Antoine, eight months off and on; Arterberry got the most and the best, three years straight.

HIGHLAND HOSPITAL The sign had been covered up for the first time in the hospital's history while shooting a movie with Richard Gere as a psychiatrist. There were cameras, dollies, and lighting equipment all around the entrance. Security, usually lax, was tight. Bern and Stacie showed their driver's licenses.

Don Milton's room in intensive care had two other patients. Bern drew the curtain for privacy.

"You still smiling, Don Milton," Bern said, kissing him, drawing back slightly. "Your forehead's so warm."

"I have this fever. I'm trying to break it. It just came on me, you know." He talked slow and barely moved.

Stacie was silent, her eyes on Don Milton. The top sheet had been pulled tight so the outline of his body was clear. His eyes opened and he turned towards Bern.

"They took it." His voice drifted off. They glanced at the slope the sheet made at the end of his torso. His right leg looked like a long tunnel next to the flatness where his left thigh had been. He moved his hands there.

"The doctors keep telling me bullshit. They can't do any more surgery. I told them, 'get it out. Get all the cancer.' I want them to get it…" His words began to slur. "Out of me. They talk shit. Run in here and talk shit. And run out."

Stacie stepped up to his side and began talking to him in a low voice. "Don Milton, I want to tell you about my trip to Aspen a few months ago. You know Aspen, Colorado?"

"Where they ski?"

"Yeah, it's real cold there. Just saying Aspen-Colorado makes me shiver. Brrrr."

He smiled faintly, then opened his eyes wide and looked at Stacie for the first time since they had come in the room

"Colder than the freezer?"

"Much colder. And you know we got to town, us black skiers – 700 strong from all over the country. 700 black people with money and plastic and attitude for the altitude."

Two small beads of sweat appeared on his forehead. He closed his eyes. "I coulda made some money."

"Oh yes. We blew into town like a cold front from Alaska. And I went right to the grocer's and you know they ain't had no grits stocked. And I said, 'Oh no, gotta be some grits in Aspen. Long as we here, get them grits on the shelves. Change up, Aspen.'"

Beads appeared. Like a sail blown by the wind, Don Milton's head listed onto his shoulder. He righted it. "Did you get your grits, Stacie?"

"You know we did. We opened up that town. And I found out how good grits taste with bottled water." He was drifting.

"Check this out, John Milton," she said loudly. He opened his eyes, "Size eight. I'll never let myself get fat."

"I can dig it," he said.

Then he motioned to Bern to bend down. He whispered, "Make her go. I have to tell you stuff."

Stacie heard him. Bern looked startled. Stacie left the room. Don Milton pushed himself up, perspiring more.

"I feel better when I sit up."

He trembled slightly. "Everything that I told you about LSD keeps coming back to me. But it's backwards, like on rewind."

"Are you dreaming about LSD?" Bern sat on the edge of the bed.

"It's not a dream. It's the medication acting on my memory, making me think about this shit over and over. First we were throwing LSD's body into the bay. Then we were laughing and watching him die. Then we were saying, Die nigguh, die. The blood was pouring out his chest like punch."

Don Milton's forehead was drenched with sweat.

"Then I stabbed him. Then I was slicing up his chest, just digging my knife in deeper and deeper. Then Loco had shot him in the back of the head. Then we had turned him around. Then he was alive again and we was talking about setting his ass up and we was all sitting around getting high. But before that I was getting mad at him."

More sweat poured down his cheeks.

"Every morning about 4:30 we would finish and count the money and put it in the pneumatic tubes and send it to Felix's building. Then LSD was talking about this time he had raped this fine sister and screwed her in the bootie and she was bleeding all on him. And she'd been a virgin and he didn't know it. And he said dammit and called her Pinky. And that was my baby sister. She was only twelve and pretty and smart in school with long hair and then she was raped and we never knew who did it and she stopped laughing and stopped going to school. And then Pinky was a baby again coming home and she was so pink we called her Pinky when she came home in the blanket."

Don Milton sank back and put his hand on Bern's wrist. He followed it as she took the tissues to his face. He closed his eyes.

"It was a good feeling. At the time. It didn't change stuff for Pinky."

"What goes around comes around, doesn't it?"

He nodded and fell back, so still she put her finger under his nose until she felt breath. She sat a few minutes until he fell asleep.

Stacie drove. Bern was quiet. Stacie broke the silence once they got on the freeway at 14th Avenue.

"I knew he was too upbeat for somebody dying of cancer."

"What the shit do you know about anything?"

"Bern, he has a morphine drip. Phil had that."

Bern cried out, looking back, in the direction of the hospital. "You are a brave nigguh and you know it, Don Milton. Take it to the bridge."

"What kind of fucking prayer is that? The man is dying."

"No, he's not." Bern began to cry.

"Yes, he is."

"No, no, no. As a man thinketh, so shall he be."

"No, he's your friend. He's going to die. This is reality. You can help him more by facing it than by pretending he's going to get well."

They passed the 35th Avenue exit. The fragrance from the eucalyptus trees shading Mills College filled the car.

"You know why I came over today without any makeup on?"

Bern looked past Stacie to the rock quarry canyon that cut through the Oakland hillside. The trucks that carried the limestone stood as if plastered to the sandy hill.

"Clifford…he doesn't have money. I mean big money… and he's on blood pressure meds."

"Are you saying he can't fuck?"

Stacie flinched but kept talking. "Bern, that's very demeaning for a man. This is a first for him and for me. I feel like I'm going on where I left off with Phil."

She inspected her face in the rear-view mirror. "We all want a prince, Bern. But the frogs are the ones leaping the fence."

"And I'm supposed to want to be like you."

"Bern, this is what I know. You think because I'm bourgeois I don't know what time it is. But I'm out here in the world like every other body, doing what Daddy told us when we were little. I keep on getting up saying good morning."

They rode in silence. Stacie took Bern's exit.

"I know this is not the right time, Stacie, but —" Bern stammered. "Don Milton. He was going to loan me the money to pay my rent. I need to ask you for $400."

"Where was he coming up with $400? You think when Felix Mitchell got stabbed to death, he became an angel looking after his henchman Don Milton. Felix is in hell and the 69th Ave. gang's glory days are over and done with. And Don Milton has a child to support, Bern, don't forget."

"He wasn't giving it to me. It was a loan." When they unloaded Bern's groceries, Stacie wrote out a check.

"At some point, Bern, reality has to set in. Life is what you make it, not what someone gives you."

The Barbers – father, sisters, and son-in-law — went as a family to Don Milton's funeral on the fifth of August. They sat in the back of the church; Don Milton was the second of eight children to die — his extended family filled the front pews. His former clients and friends the rest. Bern had spent the day before preparing gumbo and rice, a batch for her own family and one for the Miltons.

Mr. Barber, a gumbo lover from his Mississippi heart, got back to Haas first. Yellow tape was crisscrossing the front porch. He stepped over it to read the posted sign while the others were parking.

"These crackers done evicted Bern." He stepped back

over the yellow tape.

Stacie leaned over the tape, squinting. "They can't do this. She's paid up."

Mr. Barber looked in the direction of the city hall. "This is San Leandro trying to get rid of coloreds. They want it lily white again."

Clifford stepped up to the sign and said, "Bern, when did you pay your back rent?"

Bern was silent for a minute. Stacie gave her a questioning look.

"I didn't pay it. I used the money to buy tires for my car…and to live on."

Stacie shrieked, "Your car! I gave you that money to pay your rent. Are you going to sleep in your car?" She threw up her hands. "This is crazy. And this has nothing to do with being black. Bernie wants to go through life without paying for a thing."

She walked back to her car. Clifford followed. She shouted back. "She absolutely cannot stay with me."

The Lexus pulled off. Bern appealed to her father. "I can get in the back way and get my stuff out."

"Baby, you know you can stay with your momma and me." He followed her around back. "All I want is to help you get in and get the gumbo, doll."

Bern opened the back door with the key. They began to gather up clothes, shoes, toiletries, TVs, CDs, and a Tupperware bowl filled to the Snap-On brim with gumbo. It took them about ninety minutes to load the cars. No one stopped or commented.

"Follow me," Mr. Barber told Bern. He drove toward

his house, crossing over the tracks and making a left onto San Leandro Street. When he passed the turn, Bern honked but he motioned for her to stay behind him.

He drove down Davis Street, crossed over the Nimitz freeway and turned left at the Home Depot. They parked next to the Sportsmart.

"Daddy, what is so urgent that you decided to go and get it now?"

"Something for you, Bern. Lock up." He led her into the Sportsmart. "Are you curious, baby?"

"To say the least, Daddy."

They came to the end of an aisle with four domed tents on display. Mr. Barber stooped and went in one. "This is too small."

"Too small for what?" Bern's head was cocked and her eyebrows lifted.

"I heard about this in church. The reverend say if your grown children come back home because they can't handle money — and it's not the dead of winter, make them pitch a tent and see."

"See what?"

"What it's like out there with the birds and the bees."

"You're kidding me?"

He kept going in and out of the domes. "Do I look like I'm kidding you?"

She studied him as he called out the features of the biggest tent. "Sleeps eight people. 80' at the center. That's 6'8". A basketball player's height. Quick frame system. Sets up in five minutes. Oh we're cooking with hot oil now."

"I could freeze to death at night."

"Not in August in California, doll. Molded corners. Polyurethane and canvas roof. Mildew resistant. Steel frame. Polyvinyl floor. Nine by twelve. That's big. And it's fire-retardant."

He waited for her to speak. "Baby, what did you think you were going to do?"

"I don't know…Stacie has five bedrooms."

"Stacie has a new husband to deal with. Even if she didn't, you don't need to be up there living off her. When you took that $400, Bern, you took advantage of Stacie. That wasn't nice."

Bern looked around. "I don't have $149 for a tent. When did tents get expensive?"

"This is the Winnebago of tents, darling. And I'm paying." He picked up the item ticket and went to the front of the store. Bern was quiet, but the tears were flying off her cheeks. A clerk roped the package onto Mr. Barber's car.

"I guess I disappointed everyone again."

"Not me. Long as I got my gumbo, I'm fine."

SURGERY

Let me say this: surgery separates the men from the boys. I had it on my limbs: that's child's play. Your torso, that's the real deal. Talk about self-knowledge. Doctors can't prepare you for this. Once you've been opened up, it's like going in Plato's cave and coming back out. Pre-surgery = shadows on the wall. You wake up from that anesthesia and, man oh man, you are aware. Did you know after surgery you can hear and feel what's going on inside your body? I'm talking megaphone —hear, not whisper. I caught the flu a week after I had surgery and I took Nyquil, poor stupid me. I took that Nyquil in the cup. I was getting ready for bed. It took about 15 minutes to take effect. Lying in bed I felt this gang, this marching band in my chest all these tubas, xylophones and kettle drums. Am I having a heart attack? The walls of my chest reverberated. And then, like a parade, all this went marching down my gut to my stomach At that point I thought, so this is what LSD was like. But the most amazing part was my intestines. We always hear how the intestines are miles and miles. This cacophony of sensation went down around to my back, to my front, below my navel. I was wondering where the fuck *are* my intestines? It kept going, on down my thighs legs and onto the bottom of my feet. I thought, OK this is the end of it. But it started all over again, at the heart but milder, all the way through my body. And a third time and a fourth. It just got milder and then it stopped. I took that Nyquil, cursed it out and dumped it down the toilet. When I asked doctors about it, they acted dumbfounded. I've never heard that before...interesting, they remark absent-mindedly. And yet my health provider deducts $235 a month from my paycheck. And that's all doc has to say. ANATOMY & PHYSIOLOGY, you took it, remember? In all honesty, one nurse knew what I was talking about. She's the one who told me about Nyquil, a drug of choice for college kids.

WATERZOOI

On a plane for my first time to fly to L.A. for the United Black Front Conference, I used my last twenty dollars for the ticket. The Black Student Union paid my conference fee, which took care of the hotel and meals, but first came that great step from the tarmac in Oakland to the airplane. I was acting cool, but when the plane started moving I got shaky. I downed a rum and coke, felt the alcohol glide through my system. What a rush. And the leveling off sent post-orgasmic waves through the trunk of my body. The secrets people keep quiet.

The coast of California and the city and mountains of Los Angeles looked like a sixth-grade geography lesson in papier -mâché. Landing was smoother than take-off and I stepped into the city of the angels sleepy, minus sunglasses, but ready for the teddy if that was all flying was about. Two brothers from Cal State L.A. met those of us flying in from all over the state and drove us to the conference hotel downtown. L.A. was Oakland magnified twenty times. Instead of hops across town or quick drives out of the city, every move was interminable. The city of buttsore, not angels. I stayed with the students a few sessions, the plenary - but the conference was dry. They were so earnest with their mimeo proposals, binders, binders on black history and black history mimeos. I needed deliverance.

And it was there: women in the lobby dressed in African wraps instead of sundresses like mine. Dressed like identical twins, they looked alike, sounded alike. I followed them, drawn like the river in the jungle that you're supposed to follow downstream until you reach civilization. They flowed.

"Sister," they turned and addressed me. "Are you coming to US?"

I nodded, understanding US meant Ron Karenga's cultural nationalist organization. They inclined their heads and their billowy naturals tilted, airy as cotton candy. Their carved, hanging earrings shook against erect necks. Sexy. I mean, Marilyn Monroe, rise from the dead. These women put Dorothy Dandridge to shame, with their little feet strapped in leather sandals and their one-shoulders bared like brown teeth out of their wraps. I saw that they were not twins, not even blood sisters. But they were pretty and acted alike — the scurrying when they walked, the tone of voice, the way they took in my Lerner's outfit, my stride, with a glance and a little nod. What they saw supported, by contradistinction, what and who they were.

I followed them to the seminar because they flowed. I gurgled behind them like water drizzling toward an open drain. Pure hydraulics. US, Karenga's organization which the Black Panthers scorned as cultural nationalist drivel, was holding sway. It was riveting black students on white campuses, our infant intellects atop our heads, heavy as the baskets of fruits our African counterparts balanced. We were sick and tired, and tired of being sick and tired — as Marvin X had tutored us — of a system of built-in inequity, a world, a college where the moment we registered, no matter how richly we had experienced life as a black person, we had to zap it and accept the terms offered by the white world — smugness, tradition, docility. A world of hallowed halls built by white men for white men and mostly their male children. A world where we were expected to deny our virgin soil, the world we sprang from, hybrids of Africa and all the Americas, and embrace a world as naive to us as we were not to it.

A world where I was interloper.

As we approached the room, the stronger the optical illusion: women who looked alike then didn't look alike, and men who were for sure dressed alike. The look-alike-not-alike-dress-alike people began to proliferate until, in the room with podium and microphone, they were the only people I saw. A cascade of lovely brown shoulders swathed in boldly printed cloth and a platoon of beefy faces, shiny bald heads, unsmiling mouths (all other flesh buried in fatigues and army boots). Not one variation. The women were none-too-tall; I stood out like a scarecrow in outgrown clothes. The men were none too short; I stood shoulder to shoulder with most. No one spoke to me. No one approached me. Glances, yes. Eye to eye, no. *How black do I have to be? What is this, an updated paper bag test? I guess that's for US to know and me to find out.* Two of the men tested the microphone and everyone simultaneously sat down except for me and a few stragglers who rushed to their seats with a penitent air.

A speaker, unviewable, began talking about the person waiting to address us — in a distinctly damning-with-faint -praise tone:

"Before this sister came home to Watts, I guess you would say she had impressive credentials. But we here know the single most important credential is how together your mind is, not which institution put it together for you. So without any further ado, here to read a selection especially written for all the college students here and more especially for the ones who aren't here because they weren't slick enough to weasel travel funds from their colleges — Mali."

Mali! The poet I had heard at school. I hadn't heard she was a member of US, but she had the one-shouldered look. She read her selection:

Up North
what worse fate for these years
away from ourselves
our limbs full of strange
fruit from felled branches
twisted crosswise
we pray to a white house/as if a god almighty
dwelled there
its voices curse our dark past
which courses the land
blood in the body
1954 1954? 1954

When she finished, she stepped away from the podium, as if there would be no applause. There wasn't, though a few fists rose. A man said to the woman in front of me. "Her appearance is more advanced than her ideology."

I was most surprised when she sat down next to me and greeted me by name, and asked me about my Black Student Union. Then she dropped her voice to a whisper.

"These fools are archaic. Who wrote their script? Who designed these costumes? The hack that pissed out *Guess Who's Coming To Dinner?* must have dreamed up *Guess who we gonna dress up like cavemen?* Black people."

She thought like I did — this was a roomful of bad actors.

"Negroes did not set this up...somebody set US up in this."

I tried to keep my voice low too. "Why do you say that?"

"Because the women look like extras from the set of *Stormy Weather,* that's why. And cause ain't no music. White man adds music after the film is shot. We gotta have the drum from jump." Her voice had risen; people gave us dirty looks.

"Maulana's about to speak," a man said, his arms crossed like Mr. Clean.

"Let's blow," Mali said, moving deftly out of the room. I followed, a sea of unfriendly eyes on my ass. Following behind her was like running a gauntlet but I stuck in her tracks, little knight to big knight. Why did she speak before them if she knew they didn't like her and she didn't like them? When we got to the empty hallway, I shifted so violently back into my own posture, and realized how constricted I had felt in there.

"They tripped you out, didn't they?" Mali walked us towards the main lobby.

She sang a few bars of "You're in the army now." Then she started singing from Shep and the Limelighters' "Slow drag," the last few bars where the drill sergeant says, "There's a right way and a wrong way and there's my way," pointing, to the plenary session on "right way," to the hall we'd come down on "wrong way" and grabbed my arm on "my way." The flesh of her bare shoulder, smooth and warm against my forearm, held me, the sensation of it as firm as her grip.

Men at the conference were dressed one of three outfits: movement coveralls, daishiki, or army fatigues. Two men, in overalls, came up to us. One lip locked Mali. He was cute, his hair curled tight to his scalp, his ears large and well shaped, close to his head; the inner part, the seashell part, was pink-pink-carnation. A dime-sized mole on his left cheek had grouped in one spot, as if all the missing pigment had longed for its kin. I glanced away but they caught me and started laughing. I didn't know if they were laughing at me or just glad to see each other.

"This my play cousin, Howard," Mali said. That could mean anything from friendly fool to friendly fuck to spare tire boyfriend — or that he actually was as close as family. The kiss didn't give me much to go on. But it mattered because my mosquito's tweeter was tweeting away.

"And his booncoon, Will."

He also looked like the home team, like he belonged in my neighborhood. Mali began telling them about the poem-reading, how well received it wasn't. "I feel like some Mexican meat patties"

"Let's walk to the market then and get the stuff to make them."

"In your hotel room Will?" I couldn't figure out what was going on, other than that I had found the real convention.

Mali smirked. "Just follow us."

We walked out of the Biltmore and across Pershing Square. Downtown L.A. looked like a demilitarized zone, full of the rubbish of demolished buildings side by side with Indian laurel street trees and oddly incongruous pots of flowing plants.

Howard pointed to a fortress. "The Main Library." I thought of all the books inside, trapped.

"Whoa," I said as we came to a hill. "This is like San Francisco. I thought all of L.A. was flat as a board."

Howard had become the tour guide.

"This is Bunker Hill, girl. And don't try to act like you're from San Francisco. Ain't no blacks *from* there. All y'all rode a train to *get* there."

"I'm from Berkeley via Oakland."

"Vie-uh," he sneered. "Vaya con Dios, my darling."

We turned a corner. A cable car line! "Angel's Flight, 5¢ a ride." A cable car in Los Angeles, and I'd never even ridden the one in the City.

"Who's got the quarter?" Will asked. Mali fished in her pocket. Howard took it and purchased six tickets.

"What are you going to do with the extra two?" I asked.

"Don't worry your pretty little head about it." OK. He was tweeting some, too. We went up and the city spread out, not like a grand vista or Broadway of jewels, but flat like a giant pasture.

On the other side, we walked to Grand Central Public Market. My nostrils went on alert — a food bazaar, as homey as Swan's on Tenth St. in downtown Oakland, only blown up exponentially to fit L.A. Rows and rows, aisle upon aisle, booth after booth — beans, peas, lentils, spices, teas, chilies, rice in all sizes, grains, coffees from all over the Americas, enough varieties of olive oils to make Popeye's' eyes pop, Mexican food hot and ready to eat, a rolling cart with limones, Mexicanos and other tropical fruits. That was just a corner. My eyes couldn't take it all in. Howard had disappeared. I listened in awe as Mali and Will spoke Spanish and English bartering the price down for fresh tortillas, spices and tamales. She paid, and we fought our way out of the crowded arena and into the sunlight.

"Howard went to get the car," Mali said, looking for him.

"There he is." Will waved at a late-model white Mercury, a Comet Caliente. I hesitated as Will and Mali got in the backseat as if to pair me with Howard. *Her appearance is ahead of her ideology* came back at me. Was this what I wanted? Could I be this bold? Where was the me that I left behind in the City? The car seat seemed as long as a church pew between the two of us.

"Don't get shy," Howard said, patting the seat area next to him.

"How's he gonna court you if he has to cross the Grand Canyon?" Mali said.

"Howard, you playing with yourself? Gal so scared she hugging the door," Will snickered.

"If she go any more right, she be sitting on Harbor Freeway," Mali said.

"Voyeurs," I accused.

"That's right. I want to see this," Will smiled.

In between the ribbing, I was keeping an eye on the tangle of freeways, like I could tell them apart. We seemed to be going from one to another, like crossbars on a jungle gym. I had moved halfway between Howard and the door.

We talked casually: age, his 22, mine 20, his full name, Howard Lee, and mine, his school, Cal-State, L.A., his movement affiliation, SNCC, mine, BSU. We had turned into an upscale residential area — broad lawns, ranch houses, and sprinklers. Here I was in a car with not-so-complete strangers, oscillating away over some guy. What now? Jump out of the car? Vanish in thin air? Pinch myself. Was I was just daydreaming my way out of the stuffiness at the Biltmore? I thought it over. Mali was for real. I had seen her poetry in *The Journal of Black Poetry, Soulbook,* and *Negro Digest*. As if to quell my fears, Will began talking.

"I just got back from Florida A & M. Last semester. Good bye biochem lab, hello world."

"Here he comes, Will Knock-em-dead Buchanan," Howard was pulling the car into a driveway that ended in a carport attached to a house with clerestory windows. For an instant the windows looked like giant square eyes behind which machine guns might have been lurking.

The inside of the house — Howard's parents' — looked like something out of *Better Homes & Gardens*. Beamed cathedral ceiling. Grass cloth walls. Striped sofa and pillows, coppery pots, coppery teapots and buckets everywhere. Who was this guy? Who were these people I had glued onto? Who put up the sheer rayon panels folded in accordion pleats at the entry door? The mounted instruments — guitar, ukulele, banjo — on black burlap and adhered to the wall? The piano doing double-duty as room divider for the living-dining room? And, for heaven's sake, a loom? I tried to picture a black woman at the loom. It was hard.

While Howard fixed tequila, margaritas, and wine, Mali started on the Mexican meat patties. The kitchen beckoned me, with its stainless-steel facade and gleaming copper fan. Howard and Mali worked fast, like they'd done this before.

Will sat at the dining room table rolling joints.

"Baby girl, get the chili powder, cumin, oregano, and garlic salt," Mali commanded, cutting the tortillas in strips.

The birch-trimmed cabinets, opened and closed noiselessly. A riot of color from rows and rows of Stokely-Van Camp cans caught my eye with every door I opened. Tomato juice, fruit cocktail, sliced beets, wax beans, cling peaches, Bartlett pear halves, cut green beans, lima beans, sweet peas, apple sauce -bright blues, greens, yellows, reds. I was trying to figure out how colored folks fixed whole kernel white corn when Mali redirected my eye.

"The spice rack is right here, hon." she pointed to the spice rack tiled and inset. I bent down and plowed through the bottles, pulling out what satisfied the chef's desire.

She mashed the tamales with a fork and pressed them with the ground beef into four large patties, which she set under the broiler.

"Here," she said. "Do the tortillas till they're soft."

She set out a frying pan. I found oil in the cabinets and

poured some into the pan. I watched them for a few seconds, turned the fire low, and went back to the last cabinet I had opened. A recipe there intrigued me. I ran its name over my hungry tongue, "Waterzooi — a classic in Belgian cuisine."

Waterzooi. I liked that, it reminded me of *Franny and Zooey*. I liked the oyster-white countertops and the birch trim on the cabinetwork and the pass-through.

Mali called to Howard hunched over a chessboard with Will.

"I started it. You finish, Howard." He came in and looked at the meat patties on broil, the flour tortilla strips which he turned, and called through the pass-through, "Did you remember to add milk to the patties?"

"No, I did not. I don't want gas tonight, I'm going back out." They spoke like siblings. I pulled the tortilla strips out and drained them on a paper towel. Howard poured green chile sauce into a small saucepan and set it on a burner. He pulled down a Corningware dish, laid the strips in it, and stuck it in the oven.

He turned to me. "You want to see my guns after we eat?"

"I don't know. Do we have to go down in your basement?" I had a picture of an old dusty glass cabinet, splintered, set off in some dark corner.

"They're in my bedroom." The words were a magic incantation between us. He pulled out the Corningware dish and the patties. I lifted out the patties with a slotted spatula. He rearranged the tortillas so they sat seamlessly in the dish. I placed the patties each in a neat quarter square. He poured the hot green chili sauce on top. He told me where the plates and silverware were. He carried the dish in. I followed, completely comfortable. We scarfed the first helpings down, then we all got high again. When conversation surfaced, after we had pigged out, Mali looked at the two of us. Howard was eating my share. She asked me why I was letting him do that.

"I can't eat anymore," I did say. Lust had transpositioned my appetite, was left unspoken. But her internal hearing picked it up.

"Just don't get married," she said caustically.

"Married?" I said. "You're really high."

"Yeah, you guys look like you might elope. Tonight." She was high.

Will jumped in. "Uh-oh, she's turning into Queen Mojo."

"Marry for a great friendship, not a fuckship."

"Is that a poem?" I asked.

She waved me off. "I'm warning you. Don't do it. You have to be friends for it to last."

"How would you know, Mali?" Howard said. "Your buns are out here on the ship of fuck like the rest of us. Freezing to death."

"Once the passion dies down you have to be friends. Fuckship is fine. But it ain't friendship." She got on the phone setting up the rest of her night.

"Last word, Mali, last word," Howard said as she thumbed through her book.

. "Don't get stuck cleaning some pootbutt's behind with a Q-tip. Forty years and no gold watch."

Will's ride picked him up. They sailed off into the night,

Mali swirling off behind them, Howard and I standing at the door, watching the two cars drive off.

Howard turned, "I guess this is the ship of fuck." I liked the picture.

once-African kings and queens

adrift

three centuries later

on the ship of fuck

swashbuckling

in a sea of swirling shit

Howard's bedroom had been the family room, but when he got old, he told me, they gave it to him, lock, stock, and barrel. Darkened, it looked boxy, largish, with two Ionic columns near a double bed, and a bricked-over fireplace I barely made out. He showed me a gun closet built in a short wall between a corner and a door. Two cabinets lighted from the inside housed an array of rifles and hunting equipment. A Quaker Oats box held bullets, some as big as my fingers. On the side of the box, beneath the face that looked like Ben Franklin, the legend in script read: If you stood on your head, you couldn't do more for your kids.

I'd left my shoes in the living room near the striped sofa where we had started rolling. The brick floor wasn't cold or grainy like brick, I commented.

"It's vinyl tile." Howard shut the door to the built-in cabinets.

"Oh, no wonder it's not cold." Neither of us had our shoes on. Our hair was a mess though we were still dressed. Howard pulled at me, guiding me toward the middle of the room, but since I couldn't see, I used my feet to feel my way. He bent down, and a switch clicked.

In the middle of the room, a miniature train set lit up and the engine started chugging around the periphery. A secondary set of lights came on, highlighting the tracks, a church steeple, mountains, and a village square. After the train made the first revolution, lights shone and miniature townspeople appeared — a policeman, barber, postman, and a train engineer signaling with a white flag. After the second revolution, the train stopped, its motor humming. The blinking lights lost their synchronization. Instead of a monument or clump of trees, a toy gyroscope sat in the town square, spinning wildly. The townspeople walked backwards and jerked their heads backwards instead of the mechanical friendly nod.

"Watch this."

Howard flicked on a third lighting system and out of the shadows — perched in the trees, standing at the corners, holding toy M16s — black toy people appeared.

"Where did you get those?" They weren't simply townspeople in darker shades. They were entirely different. The others were all the same pink skin, round chunks of cherub faces, smiling inanely. The blacks were multicolored, wiry like guerrillas, and had stances; some knelt, some squatted, one lay flat on a building top, his rifle pointed down.

"I made it."

"But how?"

He shrugged his shoulders. "This was my senior project in high school."

"What kind of high school did you go to?"

"A school for problem kids with high IQ's. If they

could've saved our brains and thrown the rest away, they would have."

"This is incredible. I love miniature anything, especially if it moves. You just don't know."

"I know," he said. He dimmed the light till the black people were only shadows. "But it's just a toy."

With the train making revolution after revolution, we started to mix. The train made a revolution about every two minutes.

"Waterzooi," I said.

He laughed. "You eat that?"

"Never heard of it until I saw it on your kitchen cabinet."

"That's from my mother's family. She's from Brussels."

"Waterzooi." The word, its syllables, slid between us.

"It's lemon chicken soup."

He talked between strokes.

"I think that's what the people on the train are eating. Waterzooi."

"There are no people on the train," he gasped as he penetrated the deep wall. "It's a freight train."

"That's what the people in the village are eating then."

"They can't eat. They're made of plastic."

"I want them to eat Waterzooi."

"I know. You want. You want. They don't have wants."

He had an intense rhythm, much more intense than mine, but I picked up on it.

At one point he said, "They also serve who only stand and wait." We laughed so hard we fell apart and had to stop and get high again.

In that room impregnated with plastic people, plastic and real guns, the beam passing over our corkscrewed, drenched bodies every two minutes, I came about as hard as ever, howling, fusing, a spinning mass at the center of a gyroscope pointed at the sun.

I woke up in his bed, the morning sun in my face, my bra and panties on the floor. I needed air and to pee.

"Could you open a window?" I said and got up to use the bathroom. I felt like my bladder was about to burst.

"No." He sat up against the headboard, his arms crossed behind his head.

"Why? It's funky in here."

"Gingko biloba."

He repeated it. "Is that a city ordinance in L.A.?

"That's a maidenhair tree. Outside there," he pointed to the yard beyond the glass double-doors. "The man who lived here before planted the wrong kind of tree. The females bear fruit, but it's funky. He was supposed to plant a male."

"Air. Air. Please," I pleaded.

"Open the window in the bathroom."

I went to the bathroom, closing the door behind me.

"Don't close the door. How is the air going to circulate?"

At that moment I didn't care. I opened the door. A three-way mirror over the sink reflected my brown arm against the room's white-on-white. I threw down the clothes I had scooped up and sat on the toilet. It was so low I tipped over the side of it. I couldn't help peeing at the same time. I pulled myself half up, hand on the low tank. I cursed as a pool of faint yellow piss formed at my left foot. Howard came in and went to pull me up.

"What's wrong?"

"This thing is so low, I fell off."

He started to laugh but my face said don't.

"A new kind of tank," he said. "Need help?"

"Thank you, Howard, I can take a piss all by myself."

He went back out. I could tell by his shoulders, he was laughing. I tissue-wiped the floor. I sat down, practically on my haunches, like an old-timey woman getting ready to deliver a baby, and finally said good morning to my bladder. The air suction from the flush swished my pubes. It felt like the toilet was apologizing for catching me off-guard.

When Howard dropped me at the hotel later, he said, with a laugh, "You should have seen how you looked in the three-way mirror."

And watusi to you too.

I never saw him again. First plane ride. First black power conference. First one-night stand. I guess sometimes once around does it.

TRIPLETS

I'm just ahead of the police going down Telegraph in two long parallel lines to the campus. They're going to a demonstration at Cal. I'm going to Lila's Lilac Garden at the border of Oakland and Berkeley. I like Lila with her lilac dusters that she insists we wear when we're working. On 63rd St., the Alameda County sheriffs bear down so hard on their motorcycles they look like beetles, black on black on silver and black. I look up toward the Campanile on campus, down towards downtown Oakland; each way, the sidewalk's crowded. The last time I saw this was President Kennedy's motorcade.

I pass in and out of clots of bodies, squeezed between some white kids in cut off jeans, a woman in a tie-dye dress with a lhasa apso, the shopkeepers, more people walking dogs, and sundry black people. Black Berkeleyites. Small shop owners. Grew up in Oklahoma or Texas. Came here during WWII. Worked in the shipyards. Lived in rooming houses. Stayed on, saving pocket change in Mason jars. Opened businesses. Nothing big. Restaurant. Shoe repair shop. Two-cab taxi biz. Five and dime. Fresh fruit stand. Bought bungalows in Berkeley or East Oakland. Raised kids. Still getting up saying good morning like Lila.

Lila owns, runs, and counts the day's receipts. "Long ago and far away," she loves to say, or "women are big and men are small" or "Okies are education and Texas is family." I like her hairy legs. She will not shave her legs for anything. I like that she's taller than I am, a full inch. I look for Lila in the clots. Instead I see The Girls in dusters. The Girls are not really hers; they're only ten years younger than she is. She took them in when the institution shut down. She calls them The Girls, always "C'mon, Girls" or "Now, Girls." The Girls wave me down. The police have passed now. They were closer than bark on a tree. The Girls are making over a newspaper.

"Why are you chattering like magpies?" I ask.

"Miss Lila found our picture in the newspaper. We're in the news." They talk like a pair of radios tuned to slightly different frequencies. Annette and Arletta.

"I'm afraid to ask why."

"We're not in trouble, Geniece." They call me GEE-niece instead of juh-NIECE. "The newspaper says we're going to meet our sister."

Lila comes out and motions them back into the shop.

"Did you see the police, Lila?" I ask her.

"Seen police all my life," Lila says. "Nothing new under the sun."

"They're going to arrest the demonstrators. That's new."

“Police and demonstrators. Please. These motorcycles don’t compare to a battalion of horses riding your front yard. Stomping down a good crop of mustards.” She clips dead leaves from the potted plants.

Arletta shoves the paper between Lila and me. *The Berkeley Post*, the black weekly, has their picture on the first page. I read the story out loud. How Lila took them in, noting that the birth of multiple children in the Depression was a catastrophe. The Girls were farmed out, two of them to one family, the third to another.

The Girls squeal and hop around the little shop. For as long as I’ve known them, it was rumored they were triplets. It seems the parents who took the third one have died now and authorities undertook a search for the next of kin. They found Annette and Arletta through a mental retardation registry. The third girl was coming to Oakland.

“We have a sister. We knew it. We have a sister. The paper says our sister is coming to see us.”

The picture is grainy. Her name is Trissie. The Girls go on and on. Lila takes the paper and puts it under her arms, clipping stems for the church bouquets all the while.

“Now Girls, let’s wait for the moment to get excited.” They pay her no mind. She keeps arranging bromeliads for display. She turns to Arletta. “Go get me some of the small pine bark.”

Lila and Arletta make over the bromeliads, a specialty plant. Lila says she likes bromeliads because most people consider them strange and hard to grow.

“For the tillandsia, or the cryptanthus, Miss Lila?” Arletta turns to me on her way from the soil keeper. "Geniece, we're trying to make more of the puppy bromeliads. When they sprout, you can take one home as soon as the mother plant dies. O.K.?" I nod.

"But not before it dies."

"I heard you, Arletta."

"It leaves so many pups behind. But the mother dies."

"I know, Arletta."

"Miss Lila says I put my heart and soul in my bromeliads. Didn't you, Miss Lila?" Lila nods and starts in with the grapes. She puts a bunch in the freezer for an hour and rolls them in powdered sugar. She pops them right in our mouths because our hands are usually deep in dirt.

"That's right," Lila says. "Arletta puts Arletta's heart and soul into bromeliads." Childlike, Annette starts repeating our conversation: *Arletta's heart and soul heart and soul bromeliads bromeliads so many pups so many pups the mother dies mother dies bromeliads bromeliads.*

I start sweeping the floor. Lila isn't paying me to stand around with my mouth wide open and yapping. The next day I try to explain having a boyfriend to the Girls.

"Do you satisfy him?"

"I want to discuss things with him, Arletta."

"And all he wants is one thing, Geniece?" Annette says.

I shrug as if to say, who knows. I don't know if either of The Girls has had sex. I don't think so. They look like they're my age, not in their forties. Lila told me that's because of their condition. Their word for sex is *satisfied.*

"Maybe if you give him the one thing, he will discuss

the other thing. He needs *satisfied*."

"I think he would want *satisfied* over and over," Arletta says. "And over and over." They start repeating. *Satisfied.* And *over and over.*

"Girls?" They stop. "Do you know what a virgin is?"

They nod.

"I'm a virgin. And I don't want to be one any more."

"Like when you cut your hair off," Arletta says. Their eyes had widened when they saw me with a natural for the first time. Lila sends them for weekly press and curl.

"Yeah, like that." For a few days, they touched my hair as if it was fire.

They get into a nodding contest, repeating *virgin, don't want to be one anymore, virgin, don't want to be one anymore.* They don't look stupid to me. This is what they do — repeat any new word or concept, keep their pocket change in handkerchiefs. When they repeat these words, it has a different effect on me. Being a virgin has been my choice. I want to see what it's like not to have that choice. We finish the day's bouquets.

Annette says, "Go home and take a bath, Geniece. You stink."

The next week a reporter from the Oakland Tribune comes to the shop with a younger photographer. "How exactly did the two of you come here from Oklahoma in the first place?" the reporter asks The Girls. He's white, balding, with freckles covering his forearms, face and scalp. The photographer is mute as if his camera is mouth enough.

"We came here on a train, the Santa Fe," Arletta speaks up. The reporter smiles and fiddles with his pencil.

"No, I mean the circumstances," he says. I want to jump in and tell him how they got here, but I don't know. I want Lila to talk, but she is indifferent to their presence. When she told me they were coming for the story, she said she didn't care what *The Oakland Tribune* wrote. "*We made* The Post*, that's what counts, that damn* Tribune *insults my intelligence whenever it runs a story making Negroes look like buffoons.*"

"We came to Oakland because our family was here," Arletta says. They didn't have family here; I knew that much. "Our poppa came here first and sent for us."

"When was that?" the reporter writes it down.

Arletta looks at me. "When we got older."

Irritated as hell, he looks at her and then the photographer. "Jesus, this is a joke." He puts his steno pad away and walks out of the shop. "Let's get the hell out of here."

When the two get into a dusty orange Ford Fairlane up the street, Lila comes out. We stand there watching them make a U-turn and head towards downtown Oakland. Arletta and I wave, but only the photographer nods. The Girls and I giggle.

"Humph, " Lila says. "Peckerwoods."

I turn to her. "Where *did* they come from, Lila?"

"Their people in Okmulgee took care of them as long as they could. When I heard The Girls needed a home, they were on the next train. You can't be colored and alone."

The second *Tribune* story never appears. But the third Girl comes in like rain. At first a few sprinkles, then a deluge. Lila is wired that she's on the way and we all go to the Southern Pacific Depot to pick her up. We pile in Lila's Buick Skylark. Its seats are so high and filled with horsehair we float above the streets of West Oakland. Once we pass Market Street, I can feel, just barely, the railroad tracks. Annette and Arletta play on the street names. *Myrtle, the old maid. Filbert, big fat nut. Look at that Chestnut Street roasting on the open fire. Sweet Adeline.* We pass DeFremery Park with the huge Victorian house in the center. *Here come more trees. Poplar. Cypress.* Lila points out Esther's Orbit Room and Breakfast Club like we have all the time in the world, which we do since Lila is exceedingly punctual.

"Some of these places — you'd never understand what a big deal it was." Lila's voice sounds teary, like when people sing *Lift Every Voice and Sing*. "Earl Fatha Hines whipped a mean organ in Esther's."

"When you used to be young, Miss Lila?" Annette asks.

"Young my eye. When life was a grand adventure."

Lila turns onto Campbell and finds a park across the street from a hulking, granite building. Three giant arched windows across the front look like glass portals to the San Francisco skyline.

"This is it, Girls."

I don't know whether Lila is talking about the building or coming to get Trissie.

We walk single-file like ducks behind Lila into the waiting room, past six-feet-tall cast iron lampposts marked Geo. Cotter Co., South Bend, Ind. And on past sculptured fountains, stone fruits and leaves cascading down pilasters, and lintels topped with large gilt crests. There aren't any people, only oak benches and marble under our feet. The heels of our shoes make clicking sounds across the floor.

Annette walks to a pedestal. "How come this looks like

the cemetery?"

"Look, Miss Lila! Acanthus leaves way up," Arletta points to the ceiling three stories high.

"Arletta, how can you see that design from way down here?" I ask.

"Oh, my, Arletta is right. They call it Beaux Arts, Girls. It's used in many public places," Lila says, looking up.

"Like City Hall?" I ask.

"Like City Hall, Miss Geniece." Lila is not acting at all like herself today, calling me miss and getting teary about old, dilapidated West Oakland.

"We used to come in here all decked out for our beaux going off on the hog head run. The night run. We would go to the old waterfront terminal, and board the ferry to Frisco. They had an orchestra on the ferry," Lila starts humming. Annette starts saying, *Bo, Bo, little Bo peep lost her sheep, lost her sheep.*

"Can you imagine?" Lila talks over Annette. "On a ferry on the San Francisco Bay listening to a white band playing Count Basie. Oh! This California. We left the South in the dust. And after we got back on this side of the bay, our fellas would put on their porters' uniforms and we'd take their dress clothes home. Now that was grand."

The train whistles somewhere far as if it had a baritone in its steel throat.

The Girls say, "Geniece, let's go up there."

We walk out to the platform, but I stand back. The Girls stand alarmingly close to the track. Why doesn't Lila pull them back? Does she want them to fall in front of the train and be crushed to death? Lila stands next to me, holding her car keys like prayer beads, looking for the locomotive and sighing. I feel the train's rumble in the concrete beneath me like a quake. I whisper to Lila, "is this going to drive you nuts, three of them?" I think about it, about how strong she is and how she's managed the shop and The Girls so many years. As the train whistles in, she says, "Sometimes you choose your cross, sometimes it chooses you."

A stream of passengers unlike the one we're looking for pours out. It is not hard to spot Trissie. She steps out, squinting at the sun. She puts one gloved hand up to her brow and holds her bag in the other. The Girls go up to her, Arletta leading. I can't hear what Arletta is saying because her back is to me. I make a move toward them, but Lila puts a hand on my shoulder. She doesn't speak, but her body warmth says, *Let them be.* I let them, even though curiosity is killing me. I wanted to see the look on The Girls' faces when they first met her. They stand there as if time has taken a five-minute break. Then another five minutes. I can't tell who's talking. Their heads are bobbing like doll heads. I want to turn their heads around like doll heads and have them talk to me.

Finally the three of them turn and walk towards us, Trissie in the middle. Trissie has the same exact leaf brown skin, and wide-set, saucer brown eyes, same size and build. But she has on black patent heels and they're wearing flats. They're in cotton seersucker pants and white blouses. Her dress is gabardine. A wide black-patent leather belt emphasizes her waist. They look so much alike and unalike, it's altogether a shock.

She greets us, extending a gloved hand. "Miss Lila, I am so pleased to meet you." Good googa mooga, she has a Texas accent a mile wide. We walk to Lila's car. The Girls keep Trissie between them, as if she's a balloon that could fly away right in the back seat of the Skylark. I turn around as the car hits the streets of West Oakland.

Annette says, "The street names are trees, Trissie. Poplar. Cypress. Oak."

She turns to Trissie, "Why do you talk so funny, Trissie? Like Gomer Pyle?"

Arletta reaches across Trissie and pops Annette on the forearm. "She's southern. Don't make fun. I like it."

"Linden. Wood. Look, there's the 62 bus," Annette points to the bus. Trissie turns her head and looks back like it's no big thing.

"Trissie," I say, "your outfit looks fine after all that traveling."

"That's what they taught us at college. How to keep the press no matter how hot it gets. I starched and folded everything in my suitcases."

She sits back and relaxes into the seat. Her dress rides up and we can see she has on a white panty girdle. Her stockings are lighter than her skin. Annette runs her hand over the top of Trissie's knees. "Geniece dips our stockings in coffee so they match our skin."

Lila begins her interrogation. "You went to college, Trissie?"

"Yes, ma'am."

"Oh, such manners. Where, dear?"

"Lane College. It's my alma mater."

"What a treat, Trissie. Lane's choir is singing at our church."

Trissie sits up straight on the hump. "Down south — colored folks — we suck up education."

Suck up education, Annette repeats, *suck up education.*

"You went to college?" Arletta asks.

Annette repeats *suck up education, suck it up.*

"Don't look at Trissie like she has trumpets in her ears, Geniece." Arletta rolls her eyes at me.

"I'm not looking at her like anything," I turn around facing front.

Arletta asks, "Was it hard?" I turn back around. Trissie takes off her gloves finger by finger. Her nails are trimmed and polished with clear pink shellac. Primly she says, "Perseverance is the soul of success."

"Geniece said soul is a feeling," Annette says and starts singing "Soul Man" by Sam and Dave.

"I kept my nose to the grindstone."

Annette takes the ungloved hand and places it on her leg. "Look. We have the same hands."

We look at the hands while the car crosses San Pablo Avenue. It's true. All their hands are long and the joints spindly. Arletta's nails are nibbled to the quick. Annette's are short and lined at the bed with dirt from potting plants.

"A woman's nails should be neat and above all clean," Trissie says. She gives Annette a pat on the last word.

Lila says, as she turns onto Telegraph, "To each his own, my dear."

"Are you retarded like us? " Annette asks Trissie.

Arletta says quickly, "We're not retarded. I told you, we're slow."

"In the South," Trissie says, "colored are always getting labeled and then thrown in a garbage can. But I'm not retarded. Nobody threw my brain away. I bet you're not retarded either, Annette."

"Yes, I am."

"No, we're not," Arletta says.

"I like being retarded. I don't have to do as much," Annette says.

Arletta picks up Trissie's glove and runs her fingers over it. "No we're not."

"Yes, we are and I don't care." Annette begins to repeat, *nobody threw my brain away.*

"Do you want to try it on?" Trissie asks Arletta.

"I want to try them both on." Arletta pulls the glove over the palm of her hand and flexes her gloved fingers. She holds one up for us to look at, and then pulls on the other. She holds up her hands, flutters them, and folds them primly.

"Nobody in this car is retarded, okay, Annette?" Arletta says. "Not a soul."

"Geniece said soul is a feeling." Annette begins to repeat *soul is a feeling, nobody is retarded, not in this car, not a soul.* Arletta gives the gloves back to Trissie.

I'm late for Lila's church program, too late to meet them at the flower shop. I go directly to Lila's church, which is decked out as grandly as if it's Christmas. They've hung streamers with the names of the three black colleges — Lane, Houston-Tillotson and Wiley — which have sent singers for a joint chorale program. Sitting in my aisle seat I feel the waves of music, altos, sopranos, baritones, and the crescendo of the pianist mixing gospel with the classical strains of James Weldon Johnson. *In dat great gittin' up morning* makes me so happy I talk to myself like The Girls. Nonsensical phrases *I matter, we matter, I mattered, I mattering* echo in my head, mingling with the chorale pieces.

At intermission, I go with Trissie to her alma mater table. Trissie goes to the bathroom. I sign my name on the Lane College recruiter's list.

"Are you in high school or college already?" The woman behind the table asks. I proudly tell her college. She frowns slightly and I begin to tell her about my major and my grades.

"You don't pay tuition at a junior college?"

When I tell her I pay $2 a semester, she raises her eyebrow. "Are your parents alumna?"

My mouth drops open. I don't know what to say. I don't pay tuition. My grandmother raised me. I can't come up with the right answer. Some other students come up to the table and finger the brochures. She begins speaking to them, her voice lighter. I don't want to think about why she's nicer to them. *I matter.* I look down at the program.

Trissie walks up and says with a flourish to the woman, "All is not lost that is not forgotten hence." Then she extends her hand to the woman. The woman makes a slight bow with her head and rises to embrace Trissie.

"Young lady, what good things has been your lot since you left us?" the woman says. I want to correct her and say *have* not *has*.

Trissie says, "I've been working in floral design and sales, both here and in Oklahoma." I don't know if Trissie is blowing smoke out of her ears or what. She hasn't been here a week. We don't design at Lila's; we dig up dirt and mealy bugs and spray dieffenbachia and bake the dirt to kill the bacteria.

"Are you using your degree, child?" the woman asks her. "That's the important thing. Use your education to better yourself."

"I am. I assure you, I am," Trissie answers confidently.

The woman points to a stack of yearbooks. "What year did you graduate, dear?"

Trissie looks uncomfortable. She pulls her hands together and fingers the spines of the yearbooks. "My year isn't in here, I don't believe."

"Nonsense," the woman says. "We have every one from the last twenty years."

Trissie stammers, "I, uh, I..."

The woman stops everything — questions, shuffling of yearbooks, moving her god-awful brochures like a three-card monte. A silence grips the air.

"My dear, you aren't by chance a poseur?" she asks in a damning tone.

"What's that?"

"Someone claiming to be a thing they are not."

"I can't remember which year I..."

The woman cuts her off. "Nobody forgets the year they graduated. It's a matter of pride." She restacks the yearbooks and moves the brochures away from us. I want Trissie to leave the table, get away from this woman. I want to speak in loud, confident, clear tones. *I matter, she matters, you matter, we all matter.* Instead Trissie and I walk back to our seats, Trissie not speaking but holding her head so high.

The Girls ask, "Trissie, did you see your college table?"

That's the only time Trissie looks at me. If looks could kill, I would be in a coffin. "Uh huh."

The Girls ask, "Geniece, are you going to Trissie's college?" I shrug my shoulders and we listen to "I Got a Home in That Rock," Lila's favorite spiritual. Trissie refuses to look at me or even let our arms touch on the padded rail between our seats. Voices fill every space from the floor beneath our feet to the frescoes on the ceiling. Trissie hums the last stanza with them. As the choir members link hands for the final number, *Peace in the Valley,* the director motions the audience to link hands. Trissie and The Girls link hands. Trissie leaves her other hand at her side. I place my hand on it. Her skin is hot. She draws away from me. Her skin is unlike our hands that touch water and dirt often. I try again to take her hand. Trissie pulls her hand to her chest. I wait until she puts it down again and I grab it. But she won't close her fingers around mine. It doesn't matter. I clasp her stiff hand tightly with every ounce of feeling that I have. I can feel her hurt as if I had swallowed it. I want her to hear my heart saying *I matter, you matter, we matter*. The song ends and everyone gives the choirs a standing ovation. I turn to Trissie who looks at me for a second. When I see the pure hate in her eyes I feel a sharp pain.

When I come to work a few days later Lila has put Trissie on the register, something she seldom lets the Girls do.

Arletta says, with a taunting smile, "Geniece, there's nothing for you to do."

Annette says, "Go home and take a bath, Geniece, you stink."

"Do what?" It's our game. One of The Girls will say, "Do which?" But nobody answers. I look for Lila. I can hear her humming in the back.

"Trissie, can you handle it?"

"I'm good with figures. I can do it, Geniece."

Annette says, "You have to go, Geniece. Three's company, four's a crowd." Annette repeats it over and over until I correct her. Two's company, three's a crowd.

Lila's angular body fills the shop. "Is Annette right, Lila?"

"It's up to you, sweetheart," she says. She has on gardening gloves. She's been repotting. I can see there are too many bodies in here.

"Do you want to stay here, Geniece?" Lila asks.

I want Lila to say *stay here* as a command, not a question. She only asks me once. It takes a minute to feel how tiny the shop has become.

"I guess it's time for me to go."

Lila nods and I turn to leave. Annette starts clapping.

"Annette, I thought you were my friend."

"I don't want a friend. I have my sisters and Miss Lila."

Arletta gives me a hug, Annette keeps on clapping. Trissie, popping grapes into her mouth from a brown paper bag, doesn't look me in the face. I don't want to start crying. I don't want to, but I can't help it. The tears will spill out if I blink. It's important to get out quickly.

I look at the shop from outside. The Girls and Trissie

are in motion as if I had never been there. A stinging pain in the back of my throat is worse than severe thirst. It begins there and spreads. It's funny — I hate dirt and hated getting it on my hands. Lila looks up at me, shrugs and waves me on — twice, as if to say *Go, find your cross, this is mine*. It eases the aching. As I turn to walk to the bus, Arletta comes out, squat-legged, carrying a terra cotta pot of the young bromeliads.

"Here, Geniece, I can grow more pups. They take less than a month." She gives me the pot, a kiss on the cheek and a Lila-style wave, and goes back in the shop.

On the bus, a few weeks later, I scan the Oakland Post, the society chatter, church stories and wedding announcements. A picture looks familiar. Of all things, it's Lila's shop, a picture of the Girls and Trissie standing outside the flower shop. The triplets have on dresses cinched at the waist. They look regular, sexy, like the object of men's whistles.

As I start on the first paragraph, I can hear Lila read to all three of them in her deadpan voice. I start reading the story.

"After the reunion with her sister for the first time in 42 years, Arletta Kindler, 43, had a heart attack. By the time medics reached the scene, she had expired."

Expired. I'm thinking she fainted or stopped breathing for a minute or something. I let out a howl. People look at me like I might hurt them.

"Arletta died? How could that be?" I poke the newspaper as if it can answer me. "Damn! I read *The Oakland Tribune* every day. I can't believe this happened two weeks ago. Why didn't those freckle-faced, long-eared peckers have Arletta's death in it?"

Expired. I read what a Dr. Tagliablue said: "She might have been overwhelmed by the reunion with the long-lost triplet. We don't know."

I catch a transfer bus to Berkeley, crying and cursing. Crying because Arletta died and cursing under my breath because I didn't know about it. Crying because I know about it and cursing because she had to die. *Damn. 43 years old.* I take the 51 bus down Telegraph Avenue, get off at 63rd St. and walk over to the shop. I stop cold in my tracks. Shouldn't I have brought something? Flowers to a flower shop? A card of condolence? I keep going. Sometimes it's enough to show your face, Lila once said over an elaborate bouquet somebody ordered. The shop's neon sign is blinking. Lila needs to fix it. I notice the green-and -white awning has a slat missing. Lila is so busy inside she probably hasn't noticed it. I pick up a discarded gum wrapper. There's no receptacle in sight. I stand directly in front of the tinted gold window. I see The Girls and Lila. The door is ajar. I hear them talking and laughing. The dusters look like lavender lab coats. Maybe I was imagining I read about Arletta. I look harder. Lila is showing them the stems of a chrysanthemum plant. She turns and sees my face. In a startled voice she says, "Oh, Geniece. No. Don't come in."

The Girls turn and see me as I come in the door. Annette starts screaming and yelling at me. Trissie tries to calm her. Their faces — Annette's and Trissie's — are too wide and open to hide the sadness. I know for sure that Arletta is dead. I keep walking into the store but Lila motions for me to back out. I back up and Annette yells out to me in guttural sobs that sound like *teef, teef.*

"She's calling to me, Lila."

"Geniece, I'm sorry, you have to go."

"I'm sorry I didn't come sooner."

"That's not the problem, sweetie."

"I would've come before now." I hear Annette saying *thief, thief.* "What's the matter?"

Lila sighs, standing on the sidewalk, and runs her fingers through the missing slot as if some portable piece of daylight had floated by.

"Sweetheart, the Girls are accusing you of stealing."

"Lila, I would never steal from you."

"Not me," she said. "Annette says you stole something from her."

I look back at Annette. Trissie is comforting her. "I need to clear this up right away, Lila." She blocks me from going in. "Lila, I'm trying to think of what Annette could possibly think I stole. Is something missing from the handkerchiefs? I'll talk to her."

"No, she gets hysterical if she thinks of you. Please, Geniece."

"But what is it she thinks I stole from her?"

"Geniece, it's not important. Don't aggravate a situation like this."

"Is it because of Arletta's death?"

Death is the wrong word. Lila looks like I hit her. I put my arm around her. She feels bony and delicate, not like the solid Lila I knew. For the first time I understand why people use words like passed away, departed, *expired*. I take her in both arms; her heart heaving against my chest feels like a bell swinging inside her. I sing to her, *I got a home in that rock, don't you see? I got a home in that rock.* I fight my tears.

Annette comes flying out of the shop, Trissie behind her. Annette tries to pull Lila away from me. "No, no, no, don't take Miss Lila from me."

"I'm not going to take Miss Lila from you, Annette."

"Don't steal her too, Geniece." She sobs loud enough to stop cars in traffic. "Thief, you're a thief."

"Annette, what's the matter? I didn't steal from you."

"Yes, you did. You stole Arletta. You took her bromeliads and she couldn't live without them. You stole her soul. You stole Arletta's soul." She wrenches Lila away and begins her repetitions.

"Nobody can steal your soul, Annette. It's a part of you."

Lila grips my shoulder, then lets it go and goes back in the store. *Thief, thief, you stole my sister's soul, her soul, her soul*, Annette begins screeching all the words she's learned: *nobody threw my brain away heart and soul bromeliads bromeliads you stole her soul virgin virgin coffee grind stockings suck up education suck it up satisfied satisfied satisfied.* The words sound horrible, degrading, vulgar. I look at the store, but between the sun and my blurred tears I can't see a thing. I'm being banished. The tears spill out, watering the concrete. Annette's voice follows me as I cross Telegraph Avenue to catch the bus. From the curb, she blasts all of her anguish, fury and grief at me with a set of heart-piercing shrieks:

you stole Arletta's soul you stole Arletta's soul

I FIRST SAW LEROI JONES IN THE FLESH

I first saw LeRoi Jones in the flesh, at his vociferous best, at the student body funding debate. I was stone-ass surprised that he was even there. I thought of him as a Big Important Writer From The East Coast In A Tweed Coat With Books Under His Arm squirreled away from us except for class. I knew he was due to teach a class; I had even been assigned by the BSU prez to find him and his wife Sylvia an apartment, a task I failed after two weeks of walking up and down the hills of the Fillmore and the Haight with $250 cash in my purse. They ended up having to stay at the Travel-Lodge on Market St. until someone else, more on the ball, found them a pad. Some other soul got them from the airport. Forever after when I passed Travel-Lodge on the street leading to the Bay Bridge I felt mortification at failing the test. And here he was, not in his book-lined study, not surrounded by Balzac, Genet, Ionesco, or Brecht, not hunched over a Smith-Corona portable as inspiration poured from his fingertips, not on the phone long distance with some big bubba tubba negotiating another run of "Dutchman." Nope, he had left beat nihilism for black nationalism. He was with us, giving much lip to the punk-ass white boys who controlled the student body budget and wanted, for some perverse reason that I'm sure would have never occurred to them in their native Stanislaus or Siskiyou counties to pick a fight with the BSU over our altogether legitimate and defensible hiring of LeRoi. We packed the classroom for the meeting with students — black, white, Hispanic, Asian — and community people, all black and formidable. Academia's cherubs, goodbye. We drowned them, washed over them in a wave of derision. Every time they tried business as usual, we up-against-the-wall-motherfuckered them. The white boys got tired real quick of beating their heads against a united front and they grudgingly agreed to give it up. Yay us.

Yay me. Financing LeRoi meant I got financed too. LeRoi immediately set to rehearsing and performing his play "Black Mass." We were the Black Arts and Culture Troupe, we got a van, we ran up costumes at the pad, we put on shows. Within a matter of days I was the warm-up act, reading poetry. Our prez wrote a play, "Night-time is the Right Time," and we were gone, black train down the black track. LeRoi was the engine. We had an array of talent in the BSU, actors, singers, modern dancers, to supply motive force, the cars, and I, as usual, the caboose. The prez, saying I was the quintessential naysayer, gave me a part in the play, the last line which I delivered and even changed if I chose, since the clapping and the *right-ons* started just before it and nobody could hear me say squat, We took the show to colleges, centers and anyplace they'd let us in — East Palo Alto, West Oakland, Western Addition, South Berkeley, Marin City, Seaside, Hunter's Point. I felt like a little star. Maybe not a Betelgeuse or a Procyon, but one of the white dwarfs like Sirius B.

The prez' play was big fun to perform. No Romeo and Juliet here; no boy-gets girl, boy-loses girl, boy-gets her back stuff. We improvised a riot, more like man gets mad, man gets Molotov, woman throws it. The play, as written, was a one-page set of instructions like this:

PROLOGUE

A single light shines on a man off to the side mad, making a Molotov cocktail. Across the stage, dancers rise from the floor, reaching upward. Lighting goes from shadowy to bright. A voice projects:

Night time is the right time

for riot, for love

for surprising the man

Evening is our spring

If all we got is one day

Then we only have one night

Not a winter night

lonely bleak

desolate

Spring in the night

Wake up

Bloom into blackness

brothers and sisters

Burst wide open

Be/come

be/come

Yeah come hard

and then come out

Come out

Into the streets

Dance in the streets (Play "Dancing in the Streets" here)

in the streets

Fight in the streets

Run in the streets

Throw a Molotov cocktail

in the streets

Die in the streets

Live and Die in the streets

Bring this society

to its knees

in the streets

Bring LBJ to his texas

cracker barrel knees

in the streets

Bring all the traitors

in the ivory towers

into the streets

Move into the streets

Reclaim society

in the streets

Scene One

Fat mama and a sister carrying sorrow like a ball and chain beg their brother not to throw his Molotov cocktail.

Scene Two

A younger brother watches as he throws it. The police come looking for him. He hides. The mother deliberates on whether to turn her son in.

Scene Three

The police get vicious and kill him. The younger brother announces he's going to join the army. The mother approves until she finds out it's the Black Militia.

Scene Four

The mother decides she has nothing left to lose. She joins up too. A neighbor comes as she's leaving and says:

(My line)"Some people join church, I see you joined the world."

Sometimes I threw in my grandma's old favorite, "Don't let no man drag you down," changing it, if people could hear me, to "Don't let the man drag you down," or the old standby, "You can do bad by yourself." But the point of the naysayer, as LeRoi explained it to us in class, was to show that quality of self-doubt in blacks that would always accompany liberating actions, but which would be drowned out by the exulting of the people at the moment of liberation.

Once, driving back from a show, I stood in the back of the van towering over LeRoi; I held onto the rail and observed him. He had a nice funny cackle of a laugh; he was a little guy who hunched. Even standing here in my head, he's hunched in his little finely embroidered daishiki. A compact man. A nice man. Even a gentle man. He bantered, for heavens' sake. I liked him and not at all in a sexual way. Thank goodness, he didn't give off that vibe. He was short, anyway. His vibe was *Let's get going. Let's do business. Let's put on a really good show*. On-stage, on podium, he became ferocious, shrill, harsh, demanding killer-scary.

The one time I saw him mix the two personas was his last night in town, our crowning performance at the Black House in the Fillmore district. The old Victorian that we all called the Black House was the portal to black fineness. LeRoi ranted, raved, screamed; he also talked soft and tender about his wife and the baby on the way. I got the shock of my life when he pointed her out. LeRoi Jones' wife! She had foreboding eyes and was taller than I was! I had to force myself not to gape. He married up not down! But I couldn't help staring. She was pregnant, nearly due. Her belly bloomed out so perfectly pregnant you could see her enlarged belly button sticking out through the African cotton like a pacifier. I felt bad that I nearly caused her unborn child to stay in a motel. Her hair surrounded her proudness like so many twisted branches of a tree. Even with baby abloom, she retained a slim feminine curve to her dancer's figure. And she talked about California like it had a tail. She did not like California, San Francisco, the Bay Area, and by extension, us. *California niggers are out to lunch*, I heard her say loudly several times that night. She insisted on dancing and did a solo bit. My buddies and I gave each other the elbows. So supple she looked boneless, she rolled over on her bloomy stomach as if it were a bag of raked leaves. When she finished her dance, she got up and went upstairs. I heard her say, *These San Francisco niggers are trifling-ass*. Zora Neale says language is like money. Well, Sylvia Jones paid us niggardly wages that night. Grandma's old rose-jumping, hide and seek rhyme came to mind:

honey in the bee ball/I can't see y'all/all ain't hid/caint hide over

There was no hiding from her. The applause at the end of "Night Time's the Right Time" was prolonged. While they were making thunder, I mimicked Sylvia Jones:

don't wanna struggle, don't wanna work, don't wanna make real change

hummph, California hmmph

a place with a whole lotta people who wanna do nothing

white folk here cuz they made it

niggers, what's your excuse?

Of course, people saw my grumble-face but all they heard were the last few words.

HUELBO

Bobby Seale, grubby, whiskered, armed to the teeth with his cigarettes and tape-recorder, leads our indigo-bold pack through Mosswood Park at Broadway and MacArthur across from Kaiser Permanente Hospital where I was born. We are trying for a secluded spot where we can listen, safe from the FBI bugs, to a tape that Huey sent us, via his lawyer, Alex. For elusion, we shift from one grassy knoll to another, as if eight or nine black people in a very bad mood aren't cause within itself for alarm or notice.

Silence is golden.

The tape plays out Huey's tight nasalized alto. Everyone listens intently. I do too, but I'm next to Bibo, who fell in with the group at the IHOP on Telegraph where we met for breakfast. ("What are you? My shadow? You have the nerve to pop up everywhere." "Yeah, I'm a renaissance nigger.") I'm wondering: If we're so afraid of the FBI, how come any negro that takes a notion can join and not only call himself a Panther, but end up inside the inside faster than you can say Jack Robinson? I snap to attention when I hear Huey mention my name. My name comes out of the recorder like a smoke ring. I am, he says, to assume Eldridge's duties as editor-in-chief of the paper: I trust the sister; I'm familiar with her work from the paper at Oakland City College; she's a good writer; she participated in the struggle there.

Everything changes in an instant.

We leave the park. I leave everything behind and yet take it all with me, in my head where everything settles, on pages as colorful and clear as Montgomery Ward's catalogue. Underwear. Luggage. Garden furniture. RevereWare. Folding chairs. Lawnmowers. Office furniture. Motors. Knives. Guns. I see Bobby and Huey standing like sentinels in a portable classroom at City, sternly monitoring the young white Harvard history professor they hired to teach the first black history course, Kenneth Stampp's *Peculiar Institution* as text.

I see my roomies' mouths drop and then shut when I tell them my "salary." I receive $25 a week. I received $67.50 a week from *Dateline* but this $25 is paid from the people's pocketbook; it's sacred. They are paid nothing for the office work, the running around, the back and forth between the BSU and the Party that we had all done up to then. I see my editorial on Tracy Sims and the W.E.B.Dubois Club talk she gave at City College. Students had booed her for saying Negro, for being, in essence, a political naïf, neither Marxist nor socialist, just a black girl from Berkeley protesting who wound up leading a two-day sit-in, lay -in, sleep-in at the Sheraton Palace Hotel in the City in 1964. I upbraided the audience for its intolerance and bad manners. I see

Abner in the cafeteria at Oakland City, an insufferably cute Traynor twin on each arm, each one so smart their free arm is bonded to a briefcase. Abner warns me as I eat my morning cinnamon roll and juice: Did you write that editorial yourself or did the editors make you take the other side...We're going to have to talk to you about it. I thought: Talk to me? Going to have to what? What is this? Word Patrol? And who is this all-powerful we? I'm an I, not a we. Let's be second-person singular about this, you to me to you and back. I never hear from the we. At least not that we.

I see us opening the mail every day and dollar bills, so old and faded they can't even be called green, folded in scribbled notes addressed...To The Party...for my Brothers and Sisters, many anonymous, many containing checks and donations with letters of indignation, pain, relief attached. I see the telegram from Bertrand Russell, which excited everyone and which we featured prominently in the paper. I see H. Rap Brown, Stokeley's SNCC successor, submitting an article for the paper, the words my brain keeps: DO SOMETHING NIGGER IF YOU ONLY SPIT. I see Dillard, my hip, hip ex, waiting on my apartment steps my first day as editor. I think big brain, little brain, dick brain when he starts talking about his Ghia being stolen. I tell him I can't loan him the VW even for the night because now I work for the people around the clock. He lets me know he's not the least impressed: Shit gets old, even good shit, your shit too; everything gets old. He wants to come in and lord it. He's yesterday: So who you screwing in the party? No one. That's impossible, he says. As fine and neat as he is, he sounds like an old, beat up, broken down car, not sleek like his Ghia: What's the diff between screwing in the name of the revolution, he says, and servicing the quarterback on the football team? He wants me to feel like him: What's the deal? You back to jacking yourself off? You think you got a dick down there? I'm here to tell you — you don't.

I see Uncle Boy-Boy and Aunt Ola at their dinner table. I've come for money. Unashamedly. A first for me, neither a borrower nor a beggar be. Uncle Boy-Boy questions me about school. I don't want to lie. I think about the black professor, an alcoholic, in the closet. We intimidated him into giving us A's; he told us he couldn't possibly add us so late in the semester and then give us all the same high mark. But he did it even though he knew we called him fag behind his back. I think about the term papers I used from students in the African-American Students Alliance at Berkeley. I think about James Baldwin's take on love, that it doesn't begin or end the way we set it up. They hint that Buddy and Andrea, the family's golden mocha couple, have floated up shit's creek. Too bad but it's a ways from what I need right then. Aunt Ola asks me if I know that Hopalong Cassidy waved directly at Buddy, like he was a little hero, during a parade in downtown Oakland in the fifties. I nod. She tears a little. I've heard this. What difference does a fake — anyway — Hopalong Cassidy make? Did he wave some green? Did money float out of his pockets and land in Buddy's lap? I look at pictures of Corliss in her apartment in Boston where she has begun grad school. She wears her hair completely natural. Aunt Ola remarks that her hair doesn't look like such a bad grade, maybe the perm still has a residual effect. Corliss has furnished her place with Yoruba statues, befitting an anthro doctoral student.

Ola's meatloaf with its catsup covering, the au gratin potatoes from scratch I can tell, the fresh mustard greens all taste different. Either her cooking has improved or I've been eating on the run in too many soul food places. It hits me that the roots of the BPP are here. The goodwill of the black community, and its utter disgust with the occupying army called the police, is here; our relatives are our invisible members. They have sent one, like me, from every tribe to the BPP to right the system. To cut these roots would be disastrous. I rattle off my courses: Exploration in Soc Sci (bullshit); Geol (the only one I will actually cram for); Principals and Practices of Counseling (more bullshit); Special Study, Psych (utter bullshit). I see myself stopped by the young white cop: You go to State, how'd you get in; my friends want to go there, that's the place to be. Yeah, when I'm there, it's the place to be, like never, I joke, nervous about the guns he can't see, acting out Susie-q. Lying, lying, lying.

I feel shitty.

I see Uncle Boy-Boy talking: Now you all call yourselves black revolutionaries. Off the pig, you tell us. You're teaching the young people, Death to this Racist System. You're teaching yourselves to bring the system down. Kill or be killed. Give me liberty or give me death. But when the man turns on you because you've turned on him, then you want to cry foul play, and you want us to give you all our hard earned money for your beloved defense committee, for something you willfully brought on yourself. Now, I ask you, does that make much sense for me to give you my money so you can make a white lawyer rich defending you, the bail bondsmen rich and the newspaper people who love to run behind and quote you on the 6 o'clock news? I see Uncle Boy-Boy counting out $200 in twenties, tens, and fives. The bills are old, not as faded as the money pouring from the mail in the office, but the worn-out filthy lucre of my people, cousins, aunts, uncles, and relatives by blood and marriage, who've handed it to him, bill by bill. My uncle's last words as he hugs me: Niecy, are you numb or dumb, can't you see you're swimming in catastrophe?

I see my roomies gathered one night when I come in late. Augustine smokes a cigarette, which she knows is taboo on my bed. They point to the bathroom where Li-an is sobbing. They whisper the news; Li-an has broken up with Chandro-Imi. She found out, in the worst way, he was screwing around — she got vaginitus, the screwing around infection, the last straw after Chandro paid rent on an apartment across the street and moved in some other sister. Augustine says: we're being replaced, you know, by a new crop of sisters...fresh meat. The Brother-Sister Unions vs. the Black Student Union. The BSU. A degree. My courses. It all seems so far away, like foghorns. Li-an's choking wail is close though. She sounds like she's dying by strangulation and swallowing water in gulps from a garden hose at the same time. I mean to go help her but they caution me back. She told them she needed to cry. We sit there; the smoke fills my bedroom, she cries for another fifteen minutes, too long to bear. I conjure up Chandro-Imi's face but I only get his grin. Fooled ya, didn't I, it says in his silent absence. I feel shitty towards him on her behalf. She redoubles her BPP efforts.

We all do.

I see Emory and my sturdy self putting the paper together; he shows me how to hand-letter headlines, pressing out

Instatype; cut and paste, we work at ease; kind and talented, his absolute devotion to the party guides what we do; we do it all, it seems. Emory does all the drawing, I type anything handwritten that needs to go to the typesetters, and I assist with the layout. Huey, Bobby, Eldridge — give us items; speeches, addresses, position papers. Huey and Eldridge write prolifically. We use solicited articles, telegrams from the famous and notable, poetry, rally news, announcements, and quotes from the pantheon at will — Mao, Fanon, Marx, and Che. I proudly lay out a Western Union telegram from
Betty Shabazz:

> (COPY) 718APST APR 12 68 LD081L 0LB088 DL PDB TOOL MTVERNON NY 12 711A PST. BOBBY JAMES HUTTON FAMILY, CARE KATH-LEEN CLEAVERS 850 OAK St OAKLAND CALIF THE QUESTION IS NOT WILL IT BE NON -VIOLENCE VERSUS VIOLENCE BUT WHETHER A HUMAN BEING CAN PRACTICE HIS GOD GIVEN RIGHT OF SELF-DEFENSE. SHOT DOWN LIKE A COMMON ANIMAL HE DIED A WARRIOR FOR BLACK LIBERATION. IF THE GENERATION BE-FORE HIM HAD NOT BEEN AFRAID HE PERHAPS WOULD BE ALIVE TODAY. REMEMBER LIKE SOLOMON THERE IS A TIME FOR EVERYTHING. A TIME TO BE BORN, A TIME TO DIE, A TIME TO LOVE, A TIME TO HATE, A TIME TO FIGHT AND A TIME TO RETREAT. IN THE NAME OF BROTH-ERHOOD AND SURVIVAL REMEMBER BOBBY. IT

> COULD BE YOU YOUR SON YOUR HUSBAND OR YOUR BROTHER TOMORROW. CRIMES AGAINST AN INDIVIDUAL ARE OFTEN CRIMES AGAINST AN ENTIRE NATION. TO HIS FAMILY ONLY TIME CAN ELIMINATE THE PAIN OF LOSING HIM BUT MAY HE BE REMEMBERED IN THE HEARTS AND MINDS OF ALL US.   BETTY SHABAZZ

I feel comforted. She is mother to all that swirls around her fallen husband's words. We take amphetamines near deadline so we can make it. I go three days without sleep, my skin itching in spite of showers. When I shit, I cannot believe the foot and a half length of my stools. I see myself on Divisadero St. meeting the beautiful Avotcja, a wailing poet-singer-musician, who remembers my poetry readings. Only a few months past, they seem like artifacts. I have steered past them. She seems druggy. She asks me to come to her house for a sewing collective. After delivering the issue to the printer in West Oakland, I cross the bridge and take the Fell St. exit to her place. Several sisters sit around, smoking reefer and discussing the economics of joint labor, purchasing material together. I am not a seamstress. I sewed one night of sensational wraps and wind up in this set. This keeps happening to me. Why? Avotcja takes me into her bedroom. Talks. Undresses, her belly flat like a white woman's as though it was stretched across her hipbones. She hits on me. Very soft. Unlike a man. Very soft. So soft I almost miss it. When I see her perform again, her wail seems patented in comparison. My appetite is up, my weight down. I blame the bennies. I only take them on deadline. I crave my granny's sweet potato pie. I see the lonely face of the white girl Viva on one of my Berkeley runs. She lives in a studio off Telegraph, has bright red hair and sensitive, almost mournful eyes. Bibo and I drop by to pick up copy from the Peace and Freedom Party for the paper. One of our jobs together is to deal with white people. Eldridge does it on the big scale, with the media and the white mother country radicals. We have alliances from college with whites and other colored peoples, The Third World Liberation Front, the teachers' union. We stand in the middle of the room because her room is junked with papers and books, the bed is heaped, there's nowhere else for our bodies to go. She asks us: why are you the only black people who'll talk to me? We laugh but she isn't kidding. We can't tell her how contemptibly black people regard white people; she's too nice. Not pretty, though sexy enough, she seems scattered. I wonder what ordinary white women do, how they feel, when they lose their appeal. I wonder what her real name is: Barbara, Marian, Kristin. She swears it's Viva, as in viva la revolution. Like she was born in the immediate moment. Some of us were born right here and now, sprung from the top of our own heads. I stop calling all white girls Susie-q.

I see Bibo pulling the emergency brake on the VW up and all the way out of the socket. We are high as hot air balloons. We have come to score a match box. I wait in the car while he goes in to score. But he takes so long I go in. Inside the apartment, I feel something different. Is it the bare floor? Is it that there are no books, the first place I've been in months without books or book shelves? Is it the 9mm next to the stash like casual stealth? Is it the conversation, strictly centered on pricing the marijuana? Got a lid? Yeah. Kilo? Yeah. Supplier? Yeah. Why am I so bothered by the "free" joint he passes us, why not two? By his business sense, his opportunism? The People are catching hell, risking lives, dying; some of us are sacrificing school, job, and futures for this?

Shit.

I see us — my faithful roomies — piling in a car and going to open up the BPP office for the day. We open the mail and from there we split up to do our different tasks. This day we find the plate glass front window shot to hell. It looks much worse than the windshield on my VW. The Oakland Police had boys' night out at our expense. But it boomerangs. Public sympathy builds for the party exponentially. Goodwill is the invisible pillar of the party. I see the ear of the people bent to the radio talk shows where right wing rabids who call themselves communicasters fire away at the BSU and the BPP. When my friend George is appointed BPP Minister of Education, Pat Michaels goes nuts. Every time a brother hijacks a plane to Cuba, the listeners can't contain their white-hot frenzy. Michaels intones George's full name whenever he mentions him, never using pronouns, making a monster of the name: George Mason Murray. In high school, George was smart, shy, owlish. I fell out of contact with him while I went to junior college and then fell back in with him at State where he was still smart, owlish, not as shy but still the eldest of 14 children, son of a sanctified preacher. I ask him, since he's joined, why preachers' kids are the worst, the wildest, and the wickedest. I envied him because he was an English major, the subject I lacked the nerve to major in after I took one look at his papers. I chose psychology instead. I paid for my choice by repeatedly failing psychological measurements and statistics. The only thing I hate about George is his handwriting. The task of transcribing his position papers falls to me. When I show him passages, he can't even read his own writing, a mass of concentric circles. The incendiary one that set off the Reagan police: We are slaves and the only way to become free is to kill all the slave masters. Why didn't Pat Michaels' people catch the metaphor? I see the day Bibo and I are in the hallway. The flat upstairs is a BSU pad, which made for convenience. Everything is close, accessible. I hear this horrible screaming, a woman crying out. Somebody's beating up a woman. I am ready to do something to stop it. Bibo says: that's so-and-so and so-and-so, they're screwing. I don't believe him. The woman sounds as if she's in sheer agony; torture; long, piercing, intense, high -pitched sounds. You're not a screamer, I take it. Not like that. Maybe you never had it like that. I recoil. I'd be crazy to want to scream like that. But it gets me thinking. Sex was totally undercover as a child. Even if it felt totally natural to me, the point was to keep it quiet so no one would know. I wonder if screaming is a natural or learned response. Is it connected to passion or love? I want to scream and cry but with whom?

Every time I eat out, I order sweet potato pie. More sweet potato pie. I see Eldridge's dictum rolling through the party: brothers, get married so you can concentrate on revolution. The roomies and I go to Eldridge's one morning weeks before the shootout, waiting for Kathleen to come down. When she comes into the room, we see her beauty marks, the black and blue ones; this morning they're on her legs. We get the elbows to going, the eyes to rolling. Sometimes they're on her arms. Sometimes her face. I wish somebody would try to beat on me like a damn drum, I don't care how famous his ass is. This is repellent and entertaining. We talk about it casually; everyone does. In jail, after the shootout, behind glass, Eldridge says he wishes she had an automatic beating machine so she could beat herself while he's gone. This is a joke, their battles a running joke. Repellent but funny. She and I have only one run-in. She stalks in while we're putting the finishing touches on the layout. We promised the printer we'd get it to him that night. Our eyes are bennie-red, my eyelids are third-day twitching. Cavalierly, she announces that, because Eldridge is running for President of the United States on the Peace and Freedom Party ticket, we must change the front page to a banner headline, a proclamation. No, I tell her, absolutely not. She looks at me like I've lost my mind. I repeat myself, even firmer. All hell breaks loose, a Kathleen-style all hell breaking loose. She throws an intellectual temper tantrum, a Marxist shit-fit. She accuses me of a hundred kinds of error, political blasphemy. Yes, yes, I acknowledge that, but the paper is going to bed and that's that. She storms out of the flat, promising to convene the Central Committee (huelbo, et al) lickety-split. I laugh. If she could do that, she wouldn't have come here first. Getting decisions made is no snap when one part of the triumvirate is in prison, another's in jail, and a third is somewhere on the streets at any given moment, giving speeches, rallying the troops, setting up and overseeing the national explosion of sympathy, drinking bitter dog, getting, spending, laying waste and dealing with white folks. Bibo laughs, Emory chuckles, and says: Good for you. She has no idea of how much work, how many hours go into this. I don't mind all the high yellow women, over and over and over, being picked to sleep in the kings' beds, propped on the arrowhead of the revolution to speak for the people as if they had been chosen by the people instead of by a brother entranced by the taboo he breaks or the color gulch he crosses. Give me a break from high yellow hegemony. Work is work. Give credit where credit is due. I bet there are thousands like me, brown, able, consistent, dependable, loyal, conscientious, invaluable. Don't treat us like mules. When you do, we balk. And I prefer to pick instead of being picked.

I study the Sisters' Section from an early issue. I knew the editor, also from City, another fair-skinned intelligent sister. How many held this job before me? How many after me? Will this go on into perpetuity, one set of contradictions replaced by another?

The pamphlet reads:

> SISTERS UNITE. The Black Panther Party is where the BLACK MEN are. I know every black woman has to feel proud of black men who finally decided to announce to the world that they were putting an end to police brutality and black genocide. Then they were arrested even though they had not broken a law. The reason they were arrested, Sisters, is the white power structure doesn't want any brave men with guts enough to say Hell No! to the police force in self defense of their women, themselves and all our children. That's really telling the power structure like it is. Become members of the Black Panther Party for Self Defense, Sisters, We got a good thing going.

I see Wish-Woodie coming by to see me. I'm so glad we never ran into him while we were taunting the white girls walking with brothers (*Brother, we don't want to hurt you/we only want to bring you home*). He waits until I get home, talking and laughing with my roomies. Alone, he tears into me: why is Augustine wearing the earrings he made for me? Earrings, what earrings. He recalls them for me. Oh, those...we share everything. But they were personal, one-of-a-kind. I tell him about some of the programs we are instituting — free breakfast for children, free medical clinics, not as welfare but to show the people what a just society should provide its citizens. Guns? What about guns? Can't we defend ourselves? Isn't that a constitutional freedom, the right of the people to bear arms? Ten million black people against the whole world, he throws back at me, it's numerically impossible. The people's spirit is greater than the man's technology, Wish. He fears for me. My life? Not only my life but the rest of my life. I tell him about Eldridge's marriage dictum, how I seem to have protection from having to screw because I have a very specific skill.

Wish asks me: Have I ever heard of the blue laws lecture? So-called because they were bound in blue paper, a set of 45 little-enforced laws in a book by Samuel Peters: married couples have to live together or be imprisoned; every male has to have his hair cut, rounded like a cap; no one shall cross a river on Sunday except clergy; whoever publishes a lie to the prejudice of his neighbors must sit in the stocks or get 15 lashes; women can't kiss a child on the Sabbath or on fasting day.

I ask: So?

Wish says: They didn't enforce them.

If they didn't enforce them, what were they for?

Wish says: To scare you into correct behavior.

I see Wish-Woodie's passion. It is not for revolution except as it turns inside an individual. His passion for me touches me in that individual spot. I appreciate his passion for himself, for his orphaned life, for his own held up self. I don't quite have that inside me for me. It's like I kept trying to get it inserted, like shot up with the trajectory of sperm. I walk him out. Pass it on, pass it on, give me some of what you worked so hard to get, Wish, even though I know, by instinct, that it has to germinate from inside. His sense of self hurts.

Then again, this hollow feeling that only feels full with a man's fullness inside me? It's not as hollow as it was.

THE HAND

The train for the Jersey shore pulled out of Newark half-full, children squirming against the cracked leather seats and the hot, humid morning, mothers passing out snacks, and Ouida, car in the shop, her light-brown skin as tanned as her hectic hours at the newspaper allowed. Once the train left Elizabeth and Rahway all the seats were taken, and it picked up mostly white passengers from the towns and boroughs —Woodbridge, the Amboys, Matawan, and Hazlet. At Middletown, a family boarded, the children in crisp white shorts, tees and sneakers, the husky father's hand firm on the shoulder of the mother half his size. Ouida thought, *they're intact, they eat together, the mommy and daddy sleep together side by side*. The father looked at her as if sensing her disdain. Ouida pursed her lips and waited for the train to cross the Navesink River.

Behind the smile, she delved again into the vivid nightmare that had disturbed her when she tried to leave Mickey.

They had fallen asleep after an unpleasant exchange of threats at dinner. When Ouida saw a huge hand reach out of the sky as if to stop her, she tumbled out of bed screaming, scaring the life out of Mickey. They held each other like terrified children. Mickey observed that their hearts thumping loudly together sounded like, "don't leave/don't leave/ don't leave." The Hand, they called it after she told him the dream. She interpreted it as an ominous sign to stay put.

Ouida got up as the train approached Red Bank. The husky father unfolded his arms and fixed his eye on her seat, motioning his wife to take it. From the platform, under its big banner WELCOME TO RED BANK, BIRTHPLACE OF COUNT BASIE, Ouida watched as he motioned the children to the seat. He looked like a big white duck to her, the wife and kids his ducklings. Ouida stared at them until the train pulled away, recognizing that she would never see them again — and had seen enough already. She began the eight-block walk to her parents' house, talking to herself as she passed the dairy factory and the Catholic school.

"So this is what summer is. It's white, that's what it is. White, as in white cotton, white duck, white tickets to a concert in the park, white clouds, white, white, white. Blindingly white."

Her summer clearly would not be happy. Last summer had been horrid, so horrid in retrospect that when the first heavy snow came and trapped tri-state commuters in the Holland Tunnel and on the bridges for five hours, she felt, *Good, now everybody's in distress, not just me.* Snow was her kind of white, cold white.

She tested the front door to see if her mother had locked

it. It was double-locked, which meant her mother had gone to bridge club. She went in the unlocked back door and set her bag down. Methodically she walked to the front of the house, opening curtains as if she lived there now and not fifteen years ago. The simple saltbox that had marked her horizon looked different now. She appreciated how its few details dressed it up, the central chimney, the raised first story, the clapboard siding. Her parents had bought it when her father saw it on his old postal route. Sunlight streamed in on the piano, a hymnal open to "The Old Rugged Cross," the Tiffany lamp she and her father had chosen for her mother's 60th birthday, the year before he died. Ouida's great-grandmother on her mother's side had made the quilt on the wall at the turn of the century. These were her touchstones.

Two summers before, she had seen a lawyer, a woman and a post-radical type neither high-priced nor high-powered. They had established a rapport, based on having attended Rutgers as undergrads. Since Mickey didn't want the divorce, the lawyer's advice had been to follow Mickey one time and confirm her suspicions that he was spending the night with another woman. Ouida followed Mickey's Mercedes, the purchase they had argued over bitterly before and after he bought it. He headed straight for the apartment building — no zigzag, no subterfuge — parked, got out with his overnight bag, whistling and jaunty. The doorman greeted him like he lived there. She was supposed to sit all night if he didn't come back out. But she had felt such rage when she heard him whistling that she felt like smashing the windows of his prized possession with a sledgehammer. She knew she would hurt herself most if she did anything rash.
She drove home and abandoned the idea of divorce, determined

to save her money so she could simply leave. But it wasn't simple.

Ouida knew who the woman was and where she lived. Looking back, she realized her attorney had been testing her, to see if she really wanted the divorce. She found reason after reason to stay. They had a child, Rodney. He would tire of this affair. They had just bought the house and had no equity in it. How would she function with someone else? Maybe worse. Could it be worse?

Mickey had told her bluntly, "I don't want a divorce. I don't need the white man in my business. If you don't like it here, get out."

Rodney spent every summer in Willingboro with Mickey's people. One weekend before Ouida set out to see Rodney, Mickey told her, "If you go, you go alone."

Reason after reason.

Ouida fixed herself a dish of sliced Jersey pear tomatoes and went upstairs to her old room, which her mother had converted to a sewing room/guest room. She sat on the day bed, taking in the wide expanse of green lawn that began outside the house and ran through the backfield of the Catholic school, noting the shrubbery that separated the properties. It needed the trimming her father had always done.

As she ate, the New York to D.C. Metroliner whizzed past Red Bank. She thought of all the vacationing passengers. *They're happy and I'm not. Every single one of them.* Stretching out, she remembered feigning happiness under the pressure every holiday, vacation, and summer since the marriage had gone bad.

Springtime a year before, buoyed in part by the blooming trees and flowers on the Garden State Parkway, she had decided to tell her parents. But her father — Mr. Postal Administrator of the Year, Mr. Work-Work-Work — had a stroke and died on Memorial Day.

Things change, shit happens, and as the good daughter, she pushed her own plans to the back. Her brother Claude, looking stately and preoccupied, flew in for the funeral from Nairobi where he worked for the State Department, and flew back out. At one point that summer, she found herself yearning for the dark of winter and its burrowed-under, hunkered-down feeling. For the time when she could hurt and cry for what was dying in her own life. But she was stronger than she wanted to be, strong enough to carry her burden rather than put it down, not letting the toxins in her marriage leak and harm those around her.

She woke up to the smell of frying chicken, her favorite dish in her mother's wide repertoire. Ouida washed up and went down.

Marietta Carmichael, standing at the stove, looked as if someone had brushed her lightly with age. Her hair was mingled gray, her complexion the brown of an overripe peach, dotted with black moles, her small frame leaning toward a stoop. All her life she had struggled to stand erect and stretch, beside her tall husband as if she owed the world more than her five feet. Since he died, Ouida had noticed the stoop. It was as if he had been holding up her aging process. Her father had given both his children height and something else, the standard by which they measured themselves.

Ouida bent to kiss her mother and Bal à Versailles caught

in her nostrils. She knew also that her mother wore a girdle underneath her creased jeans.

"Let's have real potatoes," Ouida said. "Give Betty Crocker a break."

They fixed summer salad and potatoes topped with Ouida's yogurt, cucumber and dill curry instead of butter.

Between bites Ouida said, "It's been worse than ever between Mickey and me."

"Don't talk with food in your mouth, sweetheart. That stops the digestive process."

Ouida finished chewing. "I'm afraid for Rodney now, mother."

"Oh, Mickey loves his boy. You still haven't forgiven, have you?"

"It goes beyond forgiving, mother. He hurts me. I can't sustain it anymore."

"It's ego with the two of you." Marietta dipped the last of her salad in the dressing. "You have yet to realize a man's ego is a balloon. If you don't keep it puffed up, you've got a problem on your hands. You let the air out and this girl gets him. He goes right over to her and she puffs it up."

Marietta wiped the napkin over her lips in a delicate movement.

"He hurt me." Ouida's voice changed pitch and her mother looked at her sharply. "I can survive hurt and go on, but not damage."

"Did Mickey hit you with his fist?"

"Mother, what if he didn't? Does that mean you won't be on my side?" They began to wash and rinse the dishes.

"All men have a vice, Ouida. If it's not drinking, it's alcohol, women, something."

"Daddy didn't."

"It wasn't so much that your father didn't have a vice. He didn't have time. In my day, men had their vices but just getting a job for Negroes was so hard. Men have always done what Mickey's doing." Marietta wiped the stove and shut the broiler door firmly. "Does it bother you what he's doing, or that he's flaunting it in your face?"

"Mickey comes home on the weekends and brings his dirty laundry. And expects me to wash it."

"You should. Somebody has to be the peacemaker. You can't have two troublemakers. That's war."

"It's insanity for me to wash his dirty drawers that have been between her funky sheets."

Ouida hung dishtowels and looked around. They had done everything. "Mother, I'm getting a divorce."

She had practiced how she would react when her mother responded. But when she saw the distress on her mother's face, all it pulled up was the white family with the husky father, their crisp white clothes and clean white sneakers. Even as overbearing as the father was, she wanted what they had. When her mother flinched, she knew why the father on the train irked her. It had nothing to do with being white. He reminded her of Mickey.

"Think of Rodney, Ouida. You don't want some other woman raising your child."

"I got another lawyer, Mother. He can't take Rodney from me."

"Think about your grandchildren, sweetheart," Marietta's eyes were tearing. "If you can hang in there with Mickey and work it out, you might even have a little girl. He's going through a stage."

"He's over and done with it, Mother. I'm over and done with it. I'm going ahead this time."

"Just try, sweetheart, to endure." Marietta began crying softly.

"I have, Mother, as much as I could." The bitterness that had built up seemed solid and hard when she was in bed, alone, but the anguish in her mother's tears washed over her.

"Mums," Ouida used Rodney's name for Marietta. "If we don't divorce, one of us is going to kill the other."

They held each other, Marietta holding hardest, Ouida dry-eyed until they let go. Then she felt her own tears. Marietta stood and poured herself a glass of water from the tap. Ouida watched her try to swallow before she let out a gasp.

"Are you alright, Mother?"

"Yes, dear, I'm fine." She set the glass on the counter. "Ouida, is that why you came this weekend? To tell me this?"

"Yes, Mother. I couldn't keep it bottled inside any longer. I filed for divorce. Mickey's going to get the papers either Monday or Tuesday."

"Poor Rodney. That poor baby." Marietta washed the tears from her hands.

Ouida remembered when her mother's knuckles were dimpled and smooth instead of slightly swollen. Watching her mother fix potato salad, dice celery and pour salt straight from the box into her palm and rub her palms over the potatoes, she had wondered as a girl how her mother knew how much salt was enough, how much mustard. How much is enough?

"I'm going to the Blake's this weekend, too."

"Tonight? You're going all the way to Willingboro tonight?" Marietta looked out the window.

"No, Mother, I'll go over tomorrow."

"On Sunday. What a day to hear bad news."

Listening to the crickets that night, Ouida thought back to her first days at *The Daily Review* in Hackensack, when she had to fight for her survival in the newsroom because she was black and a woman. On her first weekend shift, during the dinner break, the news broke about the mass suicides in Guyana. First reports, 30 suicides; an hour later, the figure tripled; then into the hundreds; and so on through the night; the staff watched stunned. Nearly a thousand people dead, their lives sacrificed for somebody's blurred vision, their relatives left to explain why and how. She felt the clarifying immediacy of history, of life and death that night in the newsroom and knew why she was a reporter, why she would fight for that job.

She was fighting again, to quell the fear she felt facing tomorrow. Mickey's family had been like family to her. Raucous, earthy, plainspoken, they had taken to her, particularly Mickey's favorite, his Aunt Regina. Regina had nicknamed Ouida "giraffe" from the start because of her light skin and long neck. Though self-conscious about her height and thinness, she'd recognized the affection. From them, even more than her own parents, she had concealed what had been developing. Lied. ("We're fine up here. How're things in the sticks? Mickey's not home." "Where is my nephew? It's past time for your husband to be home. Don't tell me he's working late on Sunday evening!")

She had thought of a dozen ways to tell them, knowing in her heart there was no way to avoid it. The continuous, unrelenting, unrelieved infidelity had damaged her. Ending her marriage felt like surviving Guyana. She and Mickey and now their kin, like all the relatives of the dead in Jonestown, would bury the marriage, grieve it, be forced to revisit it on holidays and special occasions. She turned on her side to face the thought in the darkness.

Sunday morning, driving her dad's Delta 88, Ouida drove her mother to church and got on the highway to Willingboro. She had made this 45-minute trip often, either taking Rodney or bringing him back. The Blake's meant children, fun and games, Dan and Regina's Grand Central Station of a house, umpteen relatives within walking distance. There was no way the staid, quiet, bookish atmosphere at the Carmichael's could compete. She drove up to Dan and Regina's and marveled at the windows, as usual uncurtained, the living room, kitchen and dining room open to scrutiny. Even in the basement, Dan's tools hung from the walls, and nails, cans, ratchets, screws, and old motors lined the shelves, visible from the street. Dan was Regina's second husband. Nobody called him uncle, just Dan. Regina told everybody she had made sure her second husband would be a man, "not a pretty boy Floyd." Dan was balding, squat, muscular, not pretty, and not boyish.

Dan came out to greet her with a big hug. "City girl, is this gonna be one of those wham bam visits?"

Ouida heard the noise of children in the backyard. She walked to the side of the house where children splashed across the yard, playing baseball.

"Looking for your little husband, huh?" Dan had kidded her that way since he and Regina figured out Mickey was fooling around. It was a gruff kindness that Ouida never missed until she heard it again. "There he is on third. Hey, Rod," he yelled, "your mother's here."

She spotted Rodney and waved, but he was watching the pitch. The struck ball bounced into left field and Rodney ran home. As soon as he touched the plate, he turned and waved.

Dan looked at the two of them, waving and grinning. "Ouida, blow him a kiss. That'll really blow his cool."

She was happy that he was outside and not penned in a day care center or a babysitter's apartment. Once, when Rodney was five, he heard their arguing and came to her in the bedroom. He had tried to put on fingernail polish and lipstick, but had spilled the polish on the bathroom floor. She could hear his voice, as clear as if he was still five, "I'm your friend, Mommy."

Mickey hadn't heard that but saw her washing the make-up off and cursed, "I'm not letting you turn my son into a she-boy."

She walked inside where Regina was fixing Sunday dinner. "Need me to help?"

"Oh, no, Ouida. You know this was done early," motioned her to sit. "I'm not one to stay in some hot kitchen in the summer. I gets in and out early in this kind of weather."

Ouida began running water for the dishes.

"Get out of there, girl. We haven't seen you in weeks. Or is it months?" Her wide set smile opened up her pretty, diamond-shaped face. She always wore her hair in a bun — a remarkable feat because from birth Regina had one arm. Ouida had noticed the missing limb when they met, but it simply wasn't an issue with Regina who had no use for self-pity.

The living room was cool from the tree shade and Ouida sat down in a re-upholstered club chair.

"Could Reagan win again?" Regina asked with a trace of scorn in her voice. Dan and Regina loved to talk politics.

Dan laughed heartily. "She thinks Jesse Jackson's going to the White House...Ain't no cotton-picking black man winning for President in this country."

Ouida had covered Jackson for *The Review* and spoke of his symbolic importance to blacks and other downtrodden groups. She listened for Rodney as she spoke, a part of her monitoring the tone of her own voice. She wanted to be calm and not cry.

"Let it out, Ouida," Regina said.

For the second time in two days, Ouida felt a wave wash over her bitterness. Talking calmly and deliberately just wouldn't work. The minute she spoke Mickey's name, Ouida was overcome with emotion, blurting out almost everything she had told her mother. Dan sat quietly while Regina put her arm around her. Dan's twelve-year-old son, Arturo, came in from the back. He looked at Ouida, then at his father, then at his stepmother.

"What's wrong?"

"Nothing. Go back out," Dan said.

"I'm tired of playing with them. They won't go by the rules. Hi, Aunt Ouida."

The sweetness in his voice broke the last barrier. Ouida muffled the sound coming from her throat, with her hands over her mouth. Arturo went back outside.

"Let it out, sweet Sadie," Regina stubbed her cigarette and pulled Ouida's hands from her face. "Go on, let it all out. Cry your little heart out."

When Ouida finished, Regina said quietly, "I guess the Hand isn't going to scare them two together anymore."

Ouida shook her head.

"I guess," Regina said, "it served its purpose."

"I was afraid to tell you."

"We already knew," Regina put a cigarette in her mouth. Dan reached to light it.

"Mickey told you?"

"Nope. Mr. Bigmouth."

Ouida looked astonished. "Rodney? How could he know? I never talk to the lawyer when he's around."

Regina shook her head. "Children are not dummies. If he could find where you hid the *Illustrated Kama Sutra* when he was six and come down here and tell us about it, what makes you think he wouldn't listen on your calls?"

"What has Rodney been saying, Regina?"

Dan spoke up. " Rodney gives us blow-by-blow. And I do mean blow by blow."

"I filed for divorce last week."

Dan moved to the edge of the sofa. "Ouida, do you know how many black women without no man and no job like what you got want to be in your shoes?"

"Yes, I've thought about that long and hard, Dan."

Regina looked stoic. "What about my baby?"

They walked to the window and looked at the children

playing. “Are you going to take Rodney away from us?”

“You know I could never do that. Rodney has roots here.”

“Divorce is a nasty business. I’m gonna say this to you once more. I said it when you all got married. You’re one of the family as long as you’re breathing. I know full well what Mickey’s been doing. You two grown people ain’t accountable to nobody but God. Can’t nobody tell you how to live your life. But that boy is a child, and we do for our children — no matter if the momma and daddy both turn up devil dogs. And that’s my last word.”

After dinner, Ouida drove back to her mother’s with Rodney, taking the back road to Levitt Parkway.

“Auntie Regina tells me you know a lot about the divorce,” she said, keeping her eye peeled to the road for the Walgreen’s where she had to turn left.

Rodney sat in a zone of quiet as she navigated toward I -195 and drove through the dark for twenty minutes. She glanced at him in the rear view window and knew he was thinking about what he was going to say. “I asked Daddy why you had to be divorced. And Daddy said you both want to be the boss. Is that the truth?”

“Kind of.” She was watching for the Garden State Parkway exit.

“What’s going to happen to me?” The alarm in his voice caused her to tremble.

“Nothing will change, sweetie pie. Daddy is going to move out, that’s all.”

Rodney let out a shriek that so unnerved her she had to

pull onto the shoulder before the approach to the tollbooth.

"No! I don't want Daddy to leave."

"I know, sweetheart, I know." She turned to him, thinking about what she had accomplished. Leaving the marriage. Telling everyone. The pieces of her heart felt strong in daylight, but in bed she felt as fragile as an egg and empty-hearted. Maybe a bad marriage is like a cracked egg. What was spilling right then from her cracked egg was Rodney.

She reached across the seat and pulled his head to her and caressed it with her hands. "Sweetheart, we love you. You know that, don't you?"

He was crying. "But you hate each other."

"No, baby, we can't get along. It's too much fighting."

She let go and strapped him in tightly. She pulled back onto the highway.

"We have to get to Mum's, Rodney. Let's count to ten and do-re-mi."

They counted, and then went up and down the scale until their voices cracked. Ouida tossed quarters into the gaping steel mouth at each tollbooth and Rodney kept doing do-re-mi until he fell asleep. She thought: so this is destruction, the minute the ground stops shaking, rebuilding begins.

IF 9/11 HAD HAPPENED IN HARLEM, THIS WOULD BE A DIFFERENT WORLD

"A plane driven by brown men landed in the middle of the Harlem State Office Building, killing hundreds of Harlemites. And, oh my god, missing Bill Clinton by a matter of yards. What were they thinking? Does he have the luck of the Irish or what? The fire engines were late as usual. Who gets to ghetto fires on time?"

*

"So did you hear all the cursing on network TV? The fireman who saw the first plane hit said, HOLY SHIT. And the TV stations played that over and over. HOLY SHIT. HOLY SHIT. So that's it? We can curse on network TV now? What happened to the FCC's seven forbidden words that made George Carlin's career? Who cares? Holy shit? The first night David Letterman was back and talking about the attack, he said, the GODDAMN terrorists…I'm trying to figure out why this didn't happen before. Like when Kennedy was killed. OH SHIT. SOMEBODY KILLED THE FUCKING PRESIDENT. DAMN. Or like, Marilyn Monroe was discovered dead in her fucking bed, can you imagine the look on the damn coroner's face! Or like down South on the news when Martin Luther King was killed, can you hear it in real life? 'MARTIN LUTHER COON WAS KILLED. Who took that nigger out? Good. Shit. You break one rule, break em all. Just break all the rules."

*

"I'm just waiting for the news report of this white man with blood on his hands, saying, I was up in Harlem and I saw these guys standing around card tables with their heads wrapped like those ay-rabs. And they were selling incense and playing snake charmer music and it was all like a bazaar and I thought I was back in desert storm or in Afghanistan and I lost it. I couldn't help myself...But sir, what were you doing up in Harlem in your Beamer? …You were on your way home to Scarsdale…Uh-huh …with a loaded .357 magnum, sir?"

*

"How we gonna drive humvies up and Down rugged mountain slopes in Afghanistan when we can't even steer SUVs on route 80? And please don't get drivers who use their cell phones and talk with their hands at the same time. At least I know I talk with my hands unlike some people. Who use a cell phone in a car, And talk with their hands. And call themselves driving — I'm not that bad a driver"

*

"nigguz I know said they were watching the World Trade to see if nigguz was jumping out the windows. And you really couldn't tell — which was disturbing because how you know what to feel if you can't see their color?"

*

"One good thing that's happened: those reality programs are dead in the water. And I'm glad. I watched THE FEAR FACTOR this summer, thinking: this is a whole generation that grew up in a peacetime economy. Do they know these things actually happened and are happening in the south, hello, being thrown from bridges, hanging from trees.

I'm very curious as to the backgrounds of the producers and creators of these shows because they create challenges that're very close to what oppressed and ravaged populations face: Eating worms. Being dragged by ropes on the back of trucks [Hello black contestants, have you heard there's a place called Jasper, Texas? A black man was dragged to his death there. You just want that $50,000. Okay, you affirmative action dummy.]

At least on one show there was a brother. While they dropped contestants into a pit 400 rats ran all over them, I was watching bro. I was waiting for his ass to get in a pit covered with rats. But bro said: I can't go through with this. I'm from New York. I can get rats at home. He retained his dignity. He walked away with his head up high but I heard him thinking: Damn, if only it had been rabbits or squirrels or turtles, anything but rats. I gotta represent."

*

"Anybody know Eric Benet, the singer? Does he have a resemblance to Osama or what? I'm scared for Eric. So here's an open letter to Eric Everybrother.

> Dear bro
>
> Do not grow a beard
>
> Do not wear a towel on your head
>
> Do not grow an extra ten inches
>
> Do not hide out in Hollywood because all they want is a head on a stake.
>
> First we train him to be a human attack dog ...and then he turns on us
>
> Bro, watch out..."

*

“So now we’re just bomb-crazy

Bomb the terrorists. Let’s not forget they’re here.

How you gonna bomb Jersey City

You might hit the Sopranos

How you gonna bomb Paterson

The first industrial city?

How you gonna bomb Florida

a foreign country

inside a foreign country?

We *are* a foreign country

Africans Asians Europeans

squatting on Cherokee Seminole Creek Iroquis soil

How you gonna bomb Trenton?

Passaic? Newark? Camden?

Just take out New Jersey, right.

Can you smart-bomb Boston and bypass Cambridge?

Dearborn and not hit the Grosse Pointes? Fremont, California?

Oops, we nuked Silicon Valley.

Can we make a smart-bomb

With a racial profiling chip?

Technology’s a bitch, ain’t he?”

*

"And we gotta talk about these flags. I love flags. I loved the pictures of Betsy Ross sewing that flag. Even after I learned slaves were in the background sweating and bowing and scraping and weaving in the middle of the night while miss Betsy slept in her bed that they had made, I still loved the flag. It's just bred in you.

*

But I'm still scared of white people. You know, not individual white people that I know, just individual white people that don't know me. I'm scared of em. They invented Godzilla and Frankenstein and the fun house. Blacks invented the ironing board, the stoplight, blood transfusion, and the elevator, all stuff to make life easier. Who invented tear gas and bomber jets? It's the difference between can I help you & can I kill you.

*

My friend won't buy a flag. She says, "I don't buy flags or stamps with white faces. If I stand in the line at the post office to buy stamps and all they have are flag stamps, I do without. And I don't buy stamps with white faces. All these flags are frightening. These people are exhibiting crowd behavior. I get scared when white folks go along with the crowd. That's KKK behavior. This has given them a reason to do something. It's just I don't know what. They might end up dragging me behind a pick up truck because I didn't buy a flag. When I see blacks with a flag, I want to kick them and say, don't you know?"

*

And then I know Carolina who went out and bought flags for her whole office. She says the people in her neighborhood are not like the people where she works. So far she's seen one little Barbie doll flag, scotch-taped to the side of a project."

*

A LUCKY DAY

Ouida's apartment lease ran out the month after the two other black staffers left the paper. Like a nor'easter, their leaving wiped out Ouida's support systems just as her personal life bellied up. She had put off finding a new place until she filed for divorce. Her racism in real estate front-page report showed that while whites had a hard time finding an affordable apartment in pricey Bergen County, for blacks it was an Olympian feat.

Putting her furniture in storage Ouida found a room at the YWCA. Every day she made her calls at Dunkin' Donuts on Route 4 in Hackensack, calling her sources, realtors, and Pete, her editor.

Wearing her cream-colored cashmere balmacaan, she stood in the vestibule, one ear cupped against the noise of the snow trucks outside clearing the highway for the commute traffic. She shouted into the phone. A woman and a child pulled up in a brand new Toyota Previa and walked in, the child glancing up at Ouida on the phone.

"Pete, I need a few more days," Ouida said. "I still haven't found a place to stay...Have a heart, it's snowing."

Ouida thought of the black editor who left last month and gave her a sloppy kiss and parting words: "You can shoot skag in the bathroom, come out and screw one of these white boys on your desk, and they still won't fire you. You're the only chocolate left."

On their way out, the woman with the child grappled with him while trying not to spill her coffee. He spit a mouthful of doughnut on the slush-covered floor.

"Don't give my truck story to the science desk. This is local news. Pete, where's your conscience? The fucking rigs leak radioactive shit all over my towns," Ouida said.

The toddler squirmed out of a blue down parka. Before it fell onto the slush, his mother caught it. She was agile, but coffee splashed on her blue jeans and parka and on Ouida's coat. "Oh God, I'm so sorry," she said as she swiped at the coat with one of her son's mittens.

"Damn, Pete," Ouida continued, her voice edgier, "do you want me to cry? Will that get it? Why don't you try painting your ass black and find a place to stay in Bergen County?" She listened for a while.

Her voice was shrill when she talked again, "Don't try to humor me, Pete. I can't take it anymore. I'm freezing to death in Dunkin' Donuts. Some crazy lady with a brat just ruined my coat. I cannot stay at the Y one more night," she said, dropping the receiver in anger.

Both the woman and her child looked with pity at her,

and the child reached for the dangling receiver.

"The women there have all lost their minds. Do you understand me?"

The mother grabbed the receiver and covered it with her hand. "Listen. Do you need a place to stay? This is too weird; I have a furnished basement apartment that I can't rent to save my life."

She handed Ouida the receiver. "Stop bitching. Maybe you just got lucky."

"Pete," Ouida spoke into the receiver again. "Wait. This lady is talking to me about a basement apartment."

She turned from the receiver. "Who are you? And why can't you rent it?"

"My name is Iris and this is my son Saito and we live in —"

"Why can't you rent it? What's wrong with it?"

"Nothing. It's a perfect little apartment. Come see it right now. If you like it, move in. Tonight even."

Outside, through the falling snow, the traffic snaked past, the George Washington Bridge and the Manhattan skyline in the distance. Iris tied the parka hood under her son's chin.

"We should go in my car so you won't get lost," Iris suggested. They piled in the Previa, the child in the car seat in front. Iris started the motor, pumping the gas more than necessary, and turned around. "Aren't you even going to tell us your name?"

"Ouida. Ouida Blake."

"Weeda. Oh, that's pretty. Is it African?"

"No. And it's Ouida, like oo-oo-wee with one oo."

Iris left the highway and turned onto a road that hadn't been plowed yet. She had to slow down. Ouida, watching the road, said, "Your child is beautiful."

"I know. My little mutt. My husband is Japanese and I'm Italian. But the kids look Asian. My other son, Lukas, is nine."

"Saito," Ouida said, bending forward from the backseat to look at him, the parka and knit cap covering all but his eyes. Saito peered at her.

"What beautiful eyes," Ouida spoke softly.

"Half-breeds don't get the fold," Iris said matter-of-factly, as she came to a complete stop. "They have our eyes. God, I can't see a foot ahead of me. My husband Mitsuo will kill me if he comes back from Brazil and something's happened to his new van. I better try to turn around."

She turned a corner slowly.

"*Our* eyes?"

"Like you and me. Western eyes. Plastic surgery on the eyelids is big in Tokyo. Like a nose job. Chic."

Ouida pursed her lips to keep from saying anymore, her eyes on the road until the car came to a 1-1/2 story bungalow on a corner lot.

Iris announced, "This is Glen Rock."

"I know; I cover Hackensack for the paper. This is just ten minutes from the newsroom."

"I told you it's a lucky day."

A side door led to the apartment. Inside, Ouida looked around. "It's like a doll house. It's so little."

Iris took Saito who was sleep upstairs. She came back down and unwrapped her muffler and unzipped her parka. "It's not that little. Go look at the bedroom."

Ouida walked in, looked around and called out. "I'm

getting claustrophobic. It's just too small," she said, coming back into the living room.

"Even for five-fifty? Heat included, use of my laundry room and you pay electric?" There was a silence. "My husband is in Rio right now on business but this is my decision. Take it."

Sitting on a red paisley sofa, Ouida slowly opened her purse and asked, "First, last and security?"

"Just first and last. I trust you. Besides you don't have children."

Ouida looked up at Iris and laughed. "I don't? I have a son. Eleven. He lives in Willingboro with his father."

"Really? You look like a career woman, one hundred percent. But then how would I know? I'm just a wife, I don't even sell Avon."

"Does it make a difference?" Ouida said, her wallet open. "I have him every other weekend."

"No, I think it's great. You don't look like you have a child. You drive all the way to South Jersey alone?"

Ouida pulled out eleven hundred dollar bills and a fifty. "I do everything alone. It only takes 68 minutes to get there," she said, handing the money to Iris. "Fifty is for keys. I assume I'm on a month to month?"

Iris nodded. "Do you always carry cash like this?"

"Only when I know I have to find a place in one day. Being black, I have to have some kind of an edge. It's a cold world."

Iris folded the bills and tucked them into her coat pocket. "Look on the bright side. It's always warm down here."

By midnight Ouida drove back to Glen Rock, her wagon filled with clothes on hangers, books and boxes. She unloaded it all, piece by piece, as the snowstorm filled the street with light. She finished at three a.m., her body a block of ice from going in and out. She tried to fall asleep in the bedroom but couldn't. She took a pillow and blanket and stretched out on the paisley sofa. Her clothes filled the tiny space, her wordless wool, silk and knit companions, her Ann Taylor dresses, pants from Saks, jewel -colored coats and blouses. When her body stopped moving and the muscles in her arms and jaw relaxed, she lay still, waiting. She heard the furnace spitting, then the snowflakes thudding into foot-deep banks of snow. Her chest opened up like the umbrella petals of so many wild roses and thistles after a cloudburst. Tears rinsed over the rock-hard hurt, the arguments, Mickey's threats to snatch Rodney from her, their fighting in front of him, the shock that Mickey's life pulsated within her own even with the love gone. Their turbulent eleven-year marriage was a backdrop to everything, a backdrop draped now in the shroud of divorce. Her tears wet the pillowcase, and she turned the pillow over and fell off to sleep

They met outside three days later, Iris, Saito and Ouida. The piled up snow was dingy from exhaust fumes, tire treads and footprints, the sun bright, the air crisp, the storm yesterday's news.

"Don't you cook at all?" Iris asked. "You haven't used your stove since you've been here."

"How can you tell that I haven't cooked?"

"No sound, honey. When you cook, I hear it in my kitchen."

"I hate to cook."

"But what do you eat?"

"Whatever the Montclair Diner has on the menu."

"Isn't that terribly expensive?"

"Occupational hazard and it's tax-deductible."

Iris walked to her front door, Saito behind her. "Why don't you eat up here tonight? That way I'll have someone to talk to besides myself."

Ouida's reporter-eye scanned the inside of the house that was close to bedlam. Ouida walked slowly so as not to fall over toy trucks, bright red and blue blocks or the miniature men strewn around. The sturdy battered mahogany furniture, a large, worn, tweedy-brown sofa, and a tabletop Sony TV stood like anchors in the sea of toys. Saito dove in and Iris moved quickly to the kitchen as she removed her coat. She pulled out a box of Japanese rice crackers and handed one to Saito.

"Did your boss give you more vacation time?"

"No, I went to work last night. I did good to get two days."

"I thought I heard your car come in late. So you and your boss —"

"I call him my editor."

"You have a very good relationship? You scream at him often?" Iris started opening cabinets above the kitchen counter which was crammed with spice racks, blender, electric can opener, popcorn popper, crock-pot, microwave, and two rice cookers.

"Every day. And he makes twice my salary," Ouida said, looking with interest as Iris began to boil water and pull green onions out of the crisper.

"Have you eaten Japanese food before?"

"Sushi. Egg drop soup."

"In restaurants, right? Egg drop soup is Chinese, you know?"

Ouida nodded.

"This is the everyday stuff. My husband taught me how to cook it for him."

She held up the onions. "When I learned how, he refused to cook it for me. That's the Japanese male, very competent, very macho."

A boy walked into the kitchen, a look-alike of Saito.

"This is Lukas. Lukas, this is Ouida, our new tenant." He nodded at Ouida and held his head for his mother's kiss, leaving the kitchen and seating himself in front of the TV.

"He's eleven. I'm so grateful I broke down and had Saito. I never would have known that all children aren't moody. Can you chop?"

"I'm not a kitchen imbecile," Ouida said, washing her hands in a sink crowded with a dish drain, brush container with five or six different brushes and soaking pot.

Once the buckwheat noodles were in the boiling water, and the salmon-tofu balls rolled out, Iris' attention returned to Ouida's job.

"You dress like a million. I didn't know *The Bergen Review* paid so much."

"They don't. I'm dressing for my next job."

"You mean a promotion?" Iris asked, placing the fried salmon balls on lettuce leaves.

"That, too."

"I bet this Pete likes you because you're so gutsy. God,

black women are ballsy."

"If life was fair, I'd be his boss and I'd have him fired."

Iris set out bowls for wasabi and dipping. "That's not the point of women's liberation, is it?" she asked and handed four plates to Ouida.

"The only good thing is that he's never tried to hit on me. He's totally in love with his wife. Adores her. He's a love slave," Ouida said, setting the plates.

"That's a point in his favor," Iris said, rearranging the plates and setting out tiny red bowls for wasabi and blue for dipping. "I could do with a love slave."

From the living room, Lukas asked, "What's a love slave?"

"Don't listen to my conversation," Iris answered.

When they sat down to eat, both boys come to the table. The buckwheat noodles sat in separate bamboo baskets, topped with scissor-cut seaweed. The boys used chopsticks slurping the dipped noodles loudly.

Iris apologized as she served Ouida. "I'm really sorry about the food. You know, that it's not more."

"This seems like a lot to me," Ouida said, delving her chopsticks into the noodles before she gave up and picked up a salmon ball with the sticks. It dropped short of her mouth.

"Oh no," Iris said. "I have to fix Mitsuo at least five dishes and I throw in an American entree just in case. Then I sit here and hope he likes something."

Ouida watched the boys dip and slurp. "What do you do with the food he doesn't want?"

"Leftovers, lunch, you know, woman and children as human garbage pails," Iris replied.

Ouida tried the noodles again and got a long strand hanging from her mouth on the sticks. Iris slurped as loud as the boys and said, "You're supposed to slurp. That means you're enjoying it."

"I can't even get it on the chopsticks," Ouida said.

Iris got up, her mouth full. "Oh, I'm sorry, I'll get you a fork."

"No. If a 2-year old can use chopsticks, I can."

Iris handed her a fork. "You don't have to prove anything. Just eat."

"I'm going to do it, "Ouida tried again.

"You're going to give yourself a nervous breakdown," Iris said.

"Yes, but I'll be able to do it."

That Sunday morning, the paper, thick and folded with Dagwood and Blondie on the fold, lay in the snow near the street. Ouida, coming home from her shift on the overnight desk, put it on the doorstep.

Before she reached her own door, the front door opened and Iris, in a chenille robe, her long dark hair just washed, motioned Ouida to come in.

"Come in, I have to ask you something," Iris whispered, making *be quiet* gestures with her hands. "God, are you just getting in?"

"I had to work. Time and a half plus a $50 bonus for graveyard. It amounts to about $200. Is that what you had to ask me?" Ouida was tired.

"I have some good news and some bad news." Iris lowered her voice even more and stepped close enough for Ouida to catch the scent of her shampoo. "Mitsuo came home yesterday and I told him all about you. He thinks it's great but I lost the money. By any chance, have you seen it or did I drop it in your part of the house?"

Ouida stepped back, shocked. "You put it in your coat pocket."

Iris nervously blotted the water on her neck with the collar of her robe and talked on. "I looked in every pocket of my coat, my purse, the car, in Saito's room, the living room. I've looked everywhere. I'm going to be guillotined."

"When did you last see it?"

"When you gave it to me," Iris replied. "Mitsuo is going to kill me. Why am I so stupid? I feel like a piece of taffy pulled at both ends."

"If it will make you feel better, you can look downstairs. But I saw you put it in your pocket."

They went through Iris' kitchen downstairs the back way, Iris shivering on the landing as Ouida used her key and fumbled at the light switch.

"I lose everything," Iris said, flicking on the light. "It's got to be here somewhere. It can't be outside in the snow. I had taken my coat off, hadn't I?"

Iris babbled as Ouida sat down, tired and nervous, until she was struck by the sight of Ouida's clothes hanging on racks around the room.

"You have more clothes than the Queen of England. I see why you work so hard. You have to support a habit."

She pulled the chenille robe tighter around her body and

began looking under the clothes racks.

"I hope you don't think I took or stole that money from you." Her voice shook.

Iris, down on her knees searching, looked up at Ouida, astonished. "I'd never think that. You're an honest person. I have great instincts."

She stood up. "When I heard you asking your boss for more vacation time, you told him the honest bull. Nobody does that. Everybody lies."

Ouida shrugged. "I should have used a check."

"Do you think I'd let you in my home if I didn't have a good feeling about you?"

Iris dropped back down. "The money is here. I know it. It has to be. My instincts are great; my memory is the bad guy."

They went over the room with a fine-tooth comb for the next hour, interrupted by Lukas calling Iris from upstairs.

"I have to fix breakfast. Don't worry." Iris patted Ouida. "We'll find it."

Ouida stared after Iris, afraid to open her mouth for fear of the scream inside. Instead she clasped her shoulders and murmured her mantra underneath the scream: this is only temporary, this is only temporary. She sat and wrote herself a note, the kind she often placed between the last two checks in her checkbook.

> Even though I am going through something so insane I can't even believe it, I am creating a life of harmony and beauty and peace. I will allow nobody, especially some white woman from Cuckoomonga, to drive me out of my mind. This too will pass. This too will pass. It's only temporary.

At 4:30 that afternoon, Iris woke up Ouida with a knock. She carried several covered dishes. "You can stop looking, I found it."

Iris stood in the doorway, contrite. "Did I upset you? You'll never guess where I found it."

Ouida put a wet paper towel from the sink to her face. "I'm too wiped out to guess. Where?"

"In the crock-pot. It's my hiding place from the boys. I had forgotten about it." As she talked, Iris, in jeans and a fisherman's sweater, put the covered dishes on the counter. "Did I make you cry?"

Ouida shook her head.

"Good." Iris uncovered a dish. "I can't cry; something's missing inside my tear duct. Maybe that's why I am the way I am, because I can't make tears. I brought you tofu-chicken."

Ouida didn't say anything. They stood in the small kitchen for a minute in silence before Iris held out her hands.

"I know you're trying to make amends." Ouida turned away, brushing away a tear.

"I didn't mean to hurt or insult you."

"I'm still looking for a place. The Fair Housing Council — you know the one that sends out the testers — I've registered with them."

"I made you mad. I'm sorry."

"No, this whole thing has made me determined ... to go back out into the very real world and find a suitable place."

"And you haven't even met my husband. He's Japanese but you'd like him."

RESSIE

Our building super fixed our sink, then had to come back several times to get it right. San Francisco, a city full of old, old buildings and old, old, plumbing. Each time he came, the super gave Li-an this look and we couldn't figure if he thought he might try to hit on her or what. The third time he came, he took yet another long hard look and said, " You're Kaiser's girl, aren't you?"

Li-an nodded and said, "You know my dad?"

"I used to beat the black off that son of a gun. He played some mean poker. Down at Public Works, we had a game every Saturday night — all night."

He kept talking, right on under the sink. "I knew you in pigtails. The pride of your parents' eyes. Your name Philandera, after their college."

"I go by Li -an now," she said, raising her eyebrows at me.

He finished and stood. “How old you now?”

“Twenty.”

“That old, huh?” He got his bag of wrenches. “Tell your old man to stop by the next time he’s here.”

“I will.”

“Now don’t forget.”

“I won’t.”

When he left, Li-an said, “I guess I better call my folks.”

That Sunday we went to Li-an’s folks’ for dinner. When she’d called she said they’d been more relieved than mad and insisted we come out to the house. The first question her mother asked her when we walked in the house was, “How does it feel to be on your own?” I thought they were going to scrutinize me but both parents seemed to drink in her every word. They worked the post office; Li-an’s father wore blue serge because he’d worked the window at Rincon Annex that day. We’ve been having a lot of fun, she told them.

“Everybody from State lives in the Fillmore so everyone lives within about a twenty block radius,” she said.

“Are you keeping up with your school work?” her father, a big muscular man with a serious face asked. They favored; both had dimples but his showed when he frowned, Li-an’s when she laughed.

“Yes,” she lied. We barely set foot in a classroom since we moved. School was the least happening place. I was going for world record for getting high in the evening, going out, roaming the streets of the Haight and the Fillmore, mixing nightclubbing on Divisadero or Ashbury with poetry readings at Fillmore West or the Black House, going to sleep at 4:00 a.m. and getting up for

3:00 p.m. Li-an named me Rip Van Gigi.

"Li-an, we happen to know your super," her mother said, in a knowing tone of voice. I felt like sinking straight through the floor into the ceiling of the basement. "He's an old friend of your father's. He called us when you first moved in." So that's why they didn't call the police.

"You kids think you're so smart," her mother said. "I hope you graduate straight A's for all your efforts." So. He had told them about our arrivals, departures, and myriad visitors.

"And what's your major?" she asked, turning to me.

"Psychology."

"Is it now?"

My roast beef which had started to taste good, in spite of my hatred of it, tasted like crepe paper now.

"And what kind of job do you plan on getting when you graduate?" She had the friendliest way.

"I'm thinking about draft counseling."

"And what's that?"

Li-an jumped in to save me. "Rehab counseling, Momma."

The joke between us was that I would have to go into counseling draft -dodgers since it was one more way to meet men, and she would go into nursing because she had the magic healing touch. We couldn't quite share the joke.

"Well, don't forget the post office," Mr. Kaiser said.

"The post office!?" Li-an hooted. "Please, Daddy."

"A good living, benefits, and something you can retire on," he said.

"The p.o. is a plantation, Daddy," Li-an said. "Security

like the slaves had until the invention of the cotton gin. Then they were out of luck."

"The p.o. paid for all the clothes you took with you when you left," Li-an's mother said.

Li-an put her fork down. I sipped my iced tea and wanted to be able to look away but I couldn't. I knew she was about to lash them. I knew where this conversation led. One of her parents would say, "I was black before you were born." And one would say, "Yeah, I'm a good negro, a good citizen, proud of being both, too." Would one of them also say "You're looking down trouble road with all this militant talk?"

"I would puke if I had to deliver all of white society's workings, their mail, their bills, their business letters, their magazines. And for compensation, I get to look at *Playboy* magazine for free. Thank you, Mr. Charlie."

They looked as if she had slapped them. But their faces rearranged so quickly that I didn't know if I should trust my perception.

Li-an turned to me. "That's what they do on the break, look at *Playboys*. If they're not playing cards. Like slaves in the big house looking at massa's carrying-ons."

Her mother changed topics.

"You didn't hear about Ressie, did you?"

"No," Li-an said. "How's she doing?"

Her mother glanced sharply at her father. "We should wait until after dinner."

"Did she get sick or something?"

"It was in *The Chronicle*," her mother said. Getting up and walking over to the sideboard, she opened a drawer and pulled out a clipping.

"Ressie? In the paper," Li-an said. "What did she do? Rob a bank?" She turned to me and laughed. "Ressie is the most ordinary person in the world."

She began reading the clipping, which wasn't more than an inch-and-a-half of newsprint. I watched Li-an's face as she read it. She gasped and put her hand over her mouth.

"But how do they know this is Ressie?"

"We didn't cut out the story they printed the day after this one. By then they had identified her."

Li-an started to cry. "Not Ressie. Not our Ressie." Her father got up and held her face against his hip. I wondered who Ressie was and if she had been murdered or if she had jumped off the Golden Gate Bridge or if she had gotten run over by a car. They knew but it was as if I was not there, like in a horror movie or *The Twilight Zone*. Their grief passed over me, its weight like a bag of stones from the beach dripping seawater.

"Who went to get the body?" Li-an asked.

"Sister."

"Oh, not Sister," Li-an's voice was trembling. "How could she take it? Did she get hysterical? Who went with Sister?"

"Some of the brothers from the usher board," Mr. Kaiser spoke. Telling the story to me, which I wanted them to do, might cause the bag of stones to break and spill. But I wanted to know.

"May I ask how she died?" I mustered.

Li-an's mother handed me the clipping. I saw the phrases "unidentified Negro woman" and "killed herself" and "sat down on the railroad tracks." Instantly, I was bothered, unbearably so, by her being "unidentified."

"Why did they even need to print it until they knew who she was and notified her kin?" I asked, my voice trailing as I realized I was thinking out loud. I had a picture of Ressie. Uncommonly tall, her hair done up in a colored woman's pageboy and imperiously high cheekbones. I could identify her if the damn authorities couldn't or wouldn't. Or worse, didn't care.

"But why, Momma? Why would Ressie, plain Ressie, do something like that?" Li-an clung to her father's side.

"They say she had been unhappy for some time, Lianda, baby," her mother's voice softened, and then took on a tone that crisped like a piece of toast.

"Sister said she complained about feeling bad and out-of-sorts for years. But Ressie was just a complainer. She didn't have nothing to complain about. No kids to worry her to death. No man to drive her crazy. No big house to pay on and pay on till she croaked...they say we should have listened to her all those times she complained."

Li-an's mother turned to me as if I was beyond familiarity, and thus beyond grief. But I wasn't and I wanted her to stop disparaging Ressie. Ressie wouldn't like that. Ressie was a proud woman who had fallen in front of a train; she'd lost her footing in life at the wrong place. She wasn't pitiful. And I saw her clear absolutely unblemished dark brown skin. And eyebrows like mine.

Mr. Kaiser broke free of Li-an and spoke again, "Tell the girls the miracle." Our heads both swiveled toward Li -an's mother.

"Well," Li-an's mother spoke, "they said her body was a mess, just a pitiful sight for no one to see. She had, after all, sat down with her back to the train. They got a witness man who had seen her walking alongside the track an hour before. So she had thought this out."

"Tell them," Mr. Kaiser said, dead serious.

"Her face. Not a scratch on it. Not even. Said that was the Lord's way of saying she went to heaven."

Mr. Kaiser sighed and sat back down. "But they still had a closed casket," he said.

Li-an held her head between her hands. "They already had the funeral?"

Her mother spoke deliberately, as if she had been waiting all evening to say it. "Do you think they should have waited until they found you and notified you? Believe it or not, some folks don't have time for foolishness. Some of us have to work for Uncle Sam and bury the dead."

Li-an began clearing the table and I got up to help. Her mother and father leaned back. Her mother kept talking. "Next time I'm feeling bad, I want someone to say 'let me send you to the Caribbean, doll!'...you know Ressie was a muddy woman... That's what we call the Creole woman with that light skin, look like it's dirty, muddy...she thought so too...Ressie took baths with Clorox bleach...I told her one time I thought she was going to bleach herself to death... Ressie laughed at that...she could laugh. Sometime."

I heard my voice trembling but polite. I had to defend her. So what if she was light. "Maybe she wanted somebody to understand how bad she felt. Even if only for the time it took to attend her wake."

SORORS

The ten pledges stood at attention while the big sister examined their dresses with a critical white eye. Each of the ten young women wore a white wool empire-waisted jumper with a long-sleeved black silk blouse, the pledge group's chosen colors.

"Your collar has a wrinkle . . . little sister Xavi We are not only neat, we are immaculate. We have a tradition to uphold. On this campus, we have always initiated only the best, the cream of the crop. Your individual appearance, especially during pledge week, is a statement about all of us, and all of the women who have joined this sorority. Every single soror, past, present, and future is judged by your image."

Xavi's first instinct was to touch the collar she had carefully pressed. She smothered this instinct which would have been unquestionably impudent. She had heard that word enough this past week. It hadn't been the hardest week in her life, but in her 21 years, it had been as full of questions as any she had.

Why she was pledging was the primary puzzle which she was still unable to piece together. No, why wasn't she pledging? Was this not the same sorority that thirty years ago would not allow her mother to join because she couldn't pass the paper bag test at Lincoln University, though of course she couldn't single out Lincoln as the culprit since most of the Negro colleges and schools had used the same criteria for social status: light complexion, preferably of no darker shading than a paper bag. Her mother, as dark as a roasted chestnut, had tried in vain, even waited two years for a new group of sorors to change the unspoken tradition or to make an exception in her case. After all, she did possess the exceptionally keen features and long Indian straight black hair, so highly valued by the race. But Adella, as her mother preferred to Louise which she said was a graceless name, had settled for marrying a light skinned, if uneducated man, whose genes, it was practically guaranteed, would produce a child at least half as dark as she.

Xavi had been no disappointment in that respect. An artist's skillful blending from a multihued palette could not have produced a finer yellow tone with a luster that people admired. However, Adella had been at first surprised that her baby's peach yellow face had no bridge on its nose. She set about molding Xavi's nose with her forefinger and thumb every time she looked at it. She heard people compliment her baby's beauty but saw only flatness and limitation. As black as she was, Adella had thanked the heavens everyday for keen features and straight hair. But for her baby — the one who would, dammit, be able to join any socially elite group of colored folk — to have a wide nose made her flinch. With prayer and concentration she bore the other cross, a drunken husband whose instinct during the entirety of their marriage had been to ignore her. A dentist's prosthesis rectified the gap in the front of Xavi's teeth. Ballet lessons straightened her knock knees. She was a beautiful child, after all the money, time and worry. That she was extremely bright was nice in Adella's mind, but beauty would determine all. If you had asked her to tally the net gain of her own beauty, she would have looked dumbfounded. Instead she put every whit of caring into Xavi. Xavi was salvation.

I'm paying Mama back. That's it. I'm doing this for Mama. Being a soror doesn't mean a hill of beans. Xavi had told herself this all semester. She had wanted to puke at the initiation rites. Each of them had spit into a Dixie cup. Then the soror had made them each drink from it. That had been nauseating. But a conversation she had had with one of the fraternity pledges had made her feel even weaker in the knees.

He had approached her in the commons. "I got it on the Q.T. you the next president of the white and black once you go over."

"If I get over," she retorted.

"Hey, lil' sister, ain't no doubt. Beauty, brains, fineness. If they don't let you over, the white and black would lose a lot of points with the brothers." This was the same brother she had helped through elementary chemistry. Xavi sensed that he had something to say or something to ask. He was not bright academically but he was a master at manipulation.

"All right, what else is on your mind?" She looked at him unsmilingly.

He put his hand on her head. "Your mama and your papa

sho nuff gave you a pretty head of hair. Straight and black as coal."

She reached up and removed his hand. "Get to the point."

"You'd have some pretty babies, even if you married me." His laugh was hollow and mocking. Xavi tensed at the contempt in it.

"Q.T. has it," the glints in his eyes could have been crystal knives. "That the foxy president-to-be of the white and black had a baby on the strictly Q.T. and that her big sisters would be upset, why, disgraced, maybe even expelled from national if this was the absolute, verifiable truth. Can you dig it?"

An involuntary twitch. A suddenly dry throat. A soundless thud in her abdomen. Somebody knew! Somebody had found out. Adella! She wanted to pull on her mother and be protected from this sudden exposure to the cold.

"What are you talking about?" Xavi asked with a scornful air.

"Don't act dippy, everybody knows." He was trying to do her a favor; this she knew by the way his mouth was set, like he had always known. "Everybody, everybody who knows you, knows all about you. Don't you know that a secret is the only thing culled folks love to share besides food?"

Xavi gathered her books and turned away from him. He put his hand on her shoulder.

"I just wanted you to know." He walked away.

As soon as she got to her room, Xavi dialed an outside line and called Adella long distance. She related verbatim what the fraternity brother had told her.

"Now, baby, don't be too upset, that nigger might have been pulling at straws."

"But, Mama, how could he have known? Who else knew but you and me?"

There was a long pause.

"The Dean of Girls, baby."

"The Dean of Girls? How could she possibly have known?"

"Uh, I had to tell her, baby, so you couldn't have no bad mark on your record."

"Mama, I had the baby during the summer. I wasn't showing." Xavi's voice was reaching into its highest octaves. "Mama, how did the dean find out in the first place?"

"Now calm down. Remember the social worker at the home? That colored lady who was so nice to you?"

"The one who found the baby's parents?"

"Yes, dear. She thought you might need some counseling when you got back at school. Seeing as how upset you were, how you didn't want to give up the baby at first, how you was going back 'n forth between keeping the baby or giving it up. She was trying to help you, Xavi darling, that's all."

"So what did she do?"

"She wrote the Dean a letter, and sent me a copy. It was all strictly confidential."

Xavi exploded. "Strictly confidential! To the Dean of Girls! Oh my god, no wonder everybody knows. Mama, secretaries read her mail."

"But baby, once you got back to school and started pledging, you were all right. And the Dean called and told me she tore up the letter and as far as she was concerned, she had never seen it."

"No wonder I'm the laughing stock of the whole school."

"Listen, baby, without the letter, cain't nobody prove nothing."

"Mama, that's beside the point." Her voice broke. "And to let me go through pledging knowing that everybody's got my secret on the tip of their tongues."

"Are you the first pledge with a baby off somewhere? Listen to me, Xavi, there isn't a soul on earth got a record of this. No birth certificate, no proof."

"If national finds out, it's all for nothing anyway."

"I'll take national to court on that, if need be. My baby's gonna be a soror if the walls of the Supreme Court have to shake."

"Everything is messed up, Mama."

"No, baby, everything is all right."

Xavi pledged, crossing the line, acting for all the world as if it was the most important thing in the world. That night, after the parties, slightly drunk, she opened the door to her dorm room. Without skipping a step, she walked over to the window and studied the grass twelve stories below. Unfastening the gold pin, the confirmation of her belonging, from her white jumper, Xavi threw it past the ledge and slammed the window shut.

Then she went into the bathroom, removed all the bobby pins from her hair and brushed her straight black hair for a long while, careful strokes from scalp to shoulder and out. When she finished, she took the scissors and cut it all off. When she was done, she looked into the mirror and stared for a while at her flat nose, her thin wide mouth and high forehead.

The next day she mailed a package, filled with the long severed strands of hair, from the campus post office to her mother.

ANONYMITY

Mimi felt comfortable, maybe not at home but not like a fugitive from the law, whenever she walked past the gay clubs in Sacramento. She first recognized them as a comfort zone, a refuge for anonymity when she hit the Fair Oaks curve near Manzanita and saw a gay woman's bar. Not that she went in. It was for whites, like the other bars, as far as she could tell. No one glanced at her walking past, on the outer sidewalk, in the trenches. Trench feminism was what she called it. She was comfortable with it.

Mimi had felt uncomfortable the last time she had visited the Big House, as the Black Student Union had named a two-story Victorian in the Fillmore district in San Francisco. Guys were doing lines, rolling joints, watching a porno movie playing on the wall, the same brothers who had led the longest student strike in history at State and established the nation's first black studies program there, the very same brothers who had faced off the police in Hunter's Point, West Oakland and East Palo Alto, the same brothers who finagled student body funds and bought guns for the Black Panther Party, who just a decade previous had been all over sisters with naturals and averse to sisters with pressed hair. A vision of a woman's creamy white butt and pink nipples crammed the wall in the darkened room. Someone had turned off the soundtrack, so the woman's moaning and coming hard as rocks could be imagined from her mouth opening wide and her body convulsing. Miles' quintet blasted "Nefertiti" from the stereo. That was the way Mimi had learned to get high: Turn off the TV and its white noise. Keep the set on. Put Miles or Coltrane on the box and start rolling. The politics, demonstrations, rage, cries for society to explode with justice for all, had come down to this. Sex on the wall. White sex.

"Why are brothers who're supposed to be so damn hip to the ways of the white man — and so Black — playing divine music to Miss Ann's naked behind?" Mimi had protested. But no one was taken with what she had to say, as if she had become soundless as the epoch had faded.

But here on the periphery of downtown Sacramento, amid the remnants of a semi-rural and suburban area, chop shops, Goodwill's and St. Vincent de Paul secondhand stores, gas stations and citrus groves, Mimi felt safe. A whole part of the city was her safe house. She welcomed invisibility. Here, it wasn't an insult. It was as protective as eiderdown in winter, a comfort as great as her marked-up copy of *The Souls of Black Folk*, which she had co-gendered, lovingly, respectfully, for W.E.B. DuBois. In her walk, Mimi found a newspaper, *The Matriarchist*, in a bookstore that gave an anti-feminist slant to feelings that Mimi had never articulated. The problems with the feminist movement, it said, stemmed from mothers who raised their children to compete and be part of the rat race. Who needs more generals, it asked. Instead the matriarchal values of cooperation, nurturance and peace could lead to a world without war. She hadn't purchased the newspaper but stood mesmerized by the parts that made sense to her.

She walked a good two miles, towards the strange gold drawbridge that connected downtown with west Sacramento. She began going up a slight incline. Forget generals with a mother like mine. She heard her: *You can't just bump along in life. You're young. You have it all ahead of you.*

Mother, she'd replied, what I'd like to do is just get a job, go home, go to sleep, get up, shower, eat my toast, drink some juice. But her mother had been relentless.

Mimi stepped up her pace on the incline. Curse words stopped her mother cold. Can't I just…eat…sleep…shit…and fuck?

That's marvelous.

What's so marvelous about eating, sleeping, shitting, and fucking?

That you can even add fucking.

A couple on a motorcycle, a big Harley, passed Mimi. The woman had her arms wrapped around the man's waist. Mimi marveled. How silly is that? She's hanging on to him for dear life. Yet, they looked happy and untroubled in the sunlight. The woman's long red hair feathered in the wind, but the man had on a full helmet, leather jacket, chaps and boots. As they approached the Tower Bridge, he accelerated up the incline of the span. The motorcycle swerved toward the left lane, which was occupied, and then swerved back. The bike fish-tailed. The woman lost her grip and flew off. She rolled down the incline, ending inches from Mimi's feet. The driver kept on going across the bridge.

Mimi yelled, "Wait, wait, come back."

The woman's head had hit the pavement first, and she was bleeding profusely from the scalp, cheeks and mouth. Mimi screamed at the motorcyclist but he was gone. She was there. She knelt and looked around. Not one passing car stopped. The woman was moaning unaware of Mimi who didn't know what to do. As she tried to think, she cursed her Liberal Studies major. Why didn't I major in nursing? There was so much blood she couldn't tell whether the woman's eyes were open or closed.

The woman put her left hand up and Mimi took the woman's hand which closed around her wrist. The woman tried to speak but blood was in the way. A siren pierced the blue in the distance. For a few minutes, Mimi heard loud cursing and crying, the woman struggling to speak and the siren coming closer. The siren, as always, made her heart beat faster. She realized she herself was crying and cursing the man who had left behind a woman with all this blood and pain.

A California Highway Patrolman dismounted and bent down. "Ambulance's on the way. Somebody called it in from his CB... said the bike had been modified...rear suspension arm extended...for drag racing...we're tracking the cyclist right now."

The woman gripped Mimi's wrist even stronger and stopped speaking at all. The CHP said, "She's in shock now."

"I know. What can we do for her?" Mimi said. The woman's grip felt like an iron vise on her wrist. More sirens sounded.

Mimi was afraid. Keenly aware of her own unlawfulness, she felt stronger anguish for what the woman, severely injured and abandoned, was going through. As he kneeled, he picked up the two intertwined hands, a white, delicately-freckled hand and Mimi's.

"She has her wedding ring on. Guess it wasn't her husband. Did he have on a helmet?" the cop asked.

"Yes, officer. He did. She didn't."

The ambulance and emergency crews pulled up. Two paramedics brought a stretcher and began taking the woman's vital signs. They disengaged her hand from Mimi's wrist. But the woman rooted her hand around, feeling for Mimi's.

"Are you friends?" the CHP asked. Mimi shook her head.

"I was just walking and she flew off the back of the bike. Rolled down the incline."

"He must have been going pretty fast."

"I don't know."

"You came through in the clutch, then?"

"Is she going to be all right?"

Neither answered the other. One attendant placed a white gauze pad over the wound. The other placed his gloved hand over the pad and held the pressure. Without looking up, he told Mimi, "Have to hold it tight until the bleeding stops."

The medics kept tending to the woman as the officer reported to his command center. "It was a Kawasaki? Modified for burnouts? Yeah. She told us Harley."

"Don't go by what I called it" Mimi said. "I don't know motorcycles."

The officer kept replying to the radio. "CB guy called

him a suicide jockey?"

He turned to the attendants who had gotten the woman's ID from her jeans pocket. One of them gave it to the officer who radioed it in. When he finished, he turned to all of them.

"They got him at Manzanita center. Parking lot. He picked her up in a bar and said she insisted on riding with him. Said he never met her before today."

As the woman was lifted into the ambulance, the cop thanked Mimi. "They're arresting the joker for leaving the scene of an accident, and possibly DUI."

Her heartbeat had stopped pounding like Joe Louis defending his title.

The cop looked at the ambulance going down the street. Before he mounted his bike, he muttered, "Beautiful head of hair."

The ambulance sirens didn't go on blast for half a block. The distance was just enough. The cop rode off, and Mimi breathed deeply.

Judy's *Manhattan My Ass, You're In Oakland*, a collection of poetry, won the Before Columbus Foundation's 2021 American Book Award. Her semi-autobiographical novel, *Virgin Soul*, chronicled a black female in the 60s who joins the Black Panther Party [Viking, 2013]. Her *DeFacto Feminism: Essays Straight Outta Oakland* examines the intersectionality of race, gender and spirituality experienced by a black activist and feminist foot soldier.